A
DEATH
FOR A
DOCTOR

A
DEATH
FOR A
DOCTOR

E. X. Giroux

St. Martin's Press
New York

Design by Doris Borowsky

Library of Congress Cataloging-in-Publication Data

Shannon, Doris.
   A death for a doctor.

   I. Title.
PR9199.3.S49D39   1986   813'.54   86-3801
ISBN 0-312-18603-7

First Edition

10 9 8 7 6 5 4 3 2 1

This book is for
Florence Shannon Fast
and Jack J. Fast

A
DEATH
FOR A
DOCTOR

ONE

"NO," ROBERT FORSYTHE SAID.

He didn't speak explosively, in fact the monosyllable was uttered mildly but his secretary, who had been watching Chief Inspector Kepesake, transferred her attention to the barrister. To a person who did not know Forsythe well the danger signs wouldn't be apparent. But to Abigail Sanderson, who not only was Forsythe's secretary but also once had been his father's, the signs were there. His normally pale skin was now ashen, his mouth had tightened into a tense line, and, most significantly, all color had drained from his ears. He was in the grip of a tremendous fury and was quite capable of throwing both policemen bodily from his flat.

Miss Sanderson glanced back at Kepesake, wondering whether he was aware of his danger, and found that worthy placidly examining his beautifully kept nails. Everything about Adam Kepesake was beautifully kept, she decided disdainfully. From the perfectly styled hair to the gleaming handmade shoes he was a fashion plate. Not so his sergeant, however. Detective Sergeant Brummell, dubbed with the unfortunate nickname Beau, as usual

1

looked as though he had slept in his clothes and on rising
had neglected to shave or run a comb through his shaggy
hair. Once again she decided that the brains of that team
lay with the sergeant, not the chief inspector. Kepesake
was oblivious to her employer's rage but Brummell was
staring apprehensively at Forsythe.

Adjusting his silk tie, Kepesake said, "I really can't see
how you can speak for Miss Sanderson, old boy."

Forsythe's hands knotted into fists and Sergeant Brummell
said hastily, "Been admiring your collection of jade, Mr.
Forsythe. Is that Buddha the gift from Sir Amyas Dancer?"

"Of course it is," Kepesake said impatiently. "You know
that as well as I do. Sir Amyas was quite impressed with
the way Forsythe handled that nasty business for him last
year. Nice little job, old boy."

Forsythe disliked being called "old boy" almost as much
as he disliked the chief inspector. Again Brummell interceded. "You cleared that Farquson business up pretty fast
too, Mr. Forsythe. Don't know what the chief or I would
have done without you. That's why we came here tonight.
This case in Maddersley-on-Mead has got us baffled."

"Hardly, Beau," Kepesake snapped. Sitting up straighter
in his comfortable chair, he gestured. "After all, we're the
professionals. Forsythe has simply blundered into a few
cases and had incredible luck. I'll admit the newspapers
have taken him up and made him sound like Sherlock
Holmes but as a private detective—"

"I am *not* a private detective," Forsythe told him crisply.
"I'm a barrister. And to be blunt, I've no intention of leaving London and assisting you on another case." Jumping
up, he slammed a log on an already roaring fire.

Miss Sanderson inched her chair back from the hearth.
Even on this nippy October evening the heat from that

blaze was not really necessary. Forsythe's flat had excellent central heating, but perhaps it was better for her employer to slam logs around on the grate rather than use one on the chief inspector.

Kepesake, still blissfully unaware of his host's mood, was busily heaping fuel on Forsythe's inner fire. "It's not as though we're asking anything from *you*. All we want is for Miss Sanderson to go down to Maddersley, talk to the locals, pick up any bits of gossip she can, and—"

"And pretend to be the dead woman's cousin." Forsythe swung around and stood menacingly over the chief inspector. "Stay in a house where mass murder has recently taken place, be a target for some maniac who has killed four people. Let's get one thing clear, Kepesake. Sandy is not a *detective*. She's a legal secretary. Sandy wouldn't know how to take the safety off a revolver let alone engage in unarmed combat. The answer is no. Get one of your policewomen to do it."

Kepesake was finally looking apprehensive but Brummell reached up a placating hand and touched Forsythe's arm. He said slowly, "You haven't given the chief much of a chance to explain, sir. If you'd be kind enough to sit down and . . . Thank you. Now, sir, we've combed the files of women officers in the Central Bureau. Not one fits the bill. Same with female private inquiry agents. And if you want to blame someone for suggesting Miss Sanderson, blame me, not the chief. When we located the dead woman's cousin in a rest home I figured she was the same age as your secretary and even resembles her."

"And has this cousin agreed to allow another woman to masquerade as her?"

"She certainly has, sir. Her name—again that similarity—is Abigail Sanders. Miss Sanders never met either

the dead woman or her other cousin who's living in Maddersley. Some sort of family feud. But Miss Sanders is
shocked at her relatives' deaths. The idea of those kids
being murdered sickened her. Miss Sanders says we've just
got to get the bastard—" Breaking off, Brummell looked
contritely at Miss Sanderson. "Sorry about that."

"Don't be," Miss Sanderson told him. "Tell me, sergeant, if
my namesake and look-alike feels so strongly about this why
doesn't she go to Maddersley and do the detecting herself?"

Turning his long head, Forsythe gazed at his secretary.
Some color had returned to his ears and his mouth had
relaxed. "Sandy, Beau said Miss Sanders is in a rest home."

"Has a terminal disease," Brummell said. "Doctors figure
she won't last much longer. Miss Sanders has a lot of courage. Offered to do anything in her power to help. Says
she'll brief you on everything she knows about the family.
Even is willing to lend you some jewelry and other family
mementos."

Miss Sanderson cocked her neat gray head. "And she
looks like me?"

"A superficial resemblance." The chief inspector had decided it was safe to speak again. "Tall, thin, fine bones,
blue eyes, gray hair. As Beau mentioned, about the right
age too. Perhaps mid-fifties."

It was Miss Sanderson's turn to glare at Kepesake. She
resented references to her age. It was one of her few vanities.
Under her breath she used Brummell's expression. The bastard! And as usual Kepesake was wrong. Mid-fifties indeed!
Forsythe caught her eyes and grinned. At least *he* was feeling
some better. "Care for a drink, Sandy? Kepesake, Beau?"

Miss Sanderson's sherry and the chief inspector's whiskey were poured from cut crystal decanters that had been
brought up from the barrister's Sussex home. Forsythe had

to go to the kitchen for Brummell's beer. When his guests were supplied with drinks Forsythe sank back on his chair and took a sip of his own. "I think we deserve the details, Kepesake. This business about the locals. Haven't they talked to the police?"

"They talked all right. Babbled on about the Fosters. Paul Foster was a wonderful doctor. Gillian Foster was a wonderful wife and mother. The boys were wonderful children. Everyone loved them. Didn't have an enemy in the world let alone in Maddersley-on-Mead." Kepesake's deceptively kind hazel eyes glinted. "Even Mrs. Foster's sister gave us the same story. There's no way they'll open up to the police. We need someone who seems to belong, someone related to the victims. I'm certain the locals will open up to her."

Miss Sanderson gazed down into her sherry. "Perhaps they *are* telling the truth. Couldn't some deranged person have been passing through the village and murdered on impulse? Senseless killings have happened before, you know."

"The famous homicidal maniac? Not a chance. The killer was a person who knew the family, knew the house, someone the Fosters didn't fear."

"And who left one member of the family unharmed," Brummell said. "The youngest child, a baby girl, was untouched."

Without warning and despite the waves of heat from the fireplace, Miss Sanderson shivered. Adam Kepesake nodded. "I know how you feel, Miss Sanderson. Beau and I have been involved with many homicides. I thought we were fairly hardened, but this one . . . We were called in immediately, you see. Maddersley hasn't a constable but the officers from Lambert took one look and rang up the Central Bureau. When Beau and I got there nothing had been touched. It was grisly. No, that's not quite the word. Beau?"

The sergeant's shaggy head shook. "Grisly right enough but more than that. Hard to explain."

"The children?" Forsythe suggested.

"There's that, of course. Got three kiddies of my own and deaths of little ones are awful, but no. I've seen kiddies we've had to scoop into baskets and it wasn't as bad as this." Brummell gazed into the flames. "I think what got the chief and me was that it was all so . . . so cosy."

Miss Sanderson's pale blue eyes widened and Forsythe cocked his head. "A strange word to describe murder," he told the sergeant.

Kepesake banged his fist on a green tweed knee. "Exactly the right word! *Cosy.* Damnably, unbelievably cosy. An immaculate family home. Not a thing out of place. Mother in the kitchen, seated at the table, a paring knife in one hand, chopped vegetables ready for salad—a pretty young woman wearing a ruffled apron. Father at his desk in his office. In front of him an opened medical textbook, a cigar on a tray at his elbow. Two handsome little boys sitting in child-sized chairs in the living room with the television showing a children's program." Gulping the rest of his whiskey, the chief inspector extended his glass for a refill. "And all of them dead! Mrs. Foster and the boys stabbed in the backs, Dr. Foster horribly mangled. And someone moved around that house after killing them. He propped up the bodies, washed the cups and glasses, switched the television onto another channel with a long children's show that came on at eight, built up the fire . . ."

Forsythe put down the whiskey decanter and tilted the sherry one over his secretary's glass. Miss Sanderson shook her head. "Whiskey, Robby. My flesh is crawling."

"So did ours," Brummell told her somberly. "There was something in that house to make flesh creep. Something evil. And I'm not talking about ghouls or goblins. I'm talking about something that looks human but isn't. Something that's still in that village."

Handing the sergeant another foaming glass, Forsythe asked, "How can you be sure of the movements of the murderer after his victims were dead? You said the fire had been built up and—"

"Witnesses, sir. The housekeeper, Mrs. Toogood, and the doctor's nurse, Miss Sarah Ines. Both of them knew all about the family habits. Seems Mrs. Foster was a pretty indulgent mother but on one point she was strict. The boys, Arthur and Andrew, had early suppers, were allowed to watch cartoons on the television from six to seven, and then were sent up to bed.

"Nurse Ines and Mrs. Toogood left within minutes of each other, shortly after five. At that time the boys were in the kitchen being given supper by Mrs. Foster. The parents usually dined around eight but that evening they were dining at seven because the next day was Arthur's fifth birthday and Mrs. Foster planned to do baking and so on for the party. Before Mrs. Toogood left she lit the fire in the living room."

Brummell took a long drink of beer and ran a handkerchief over his lips. "The murders were discovered by Mrs. Foster's sister, Irene Markham, a few minutes past nine. According to the police surgeon the deaths had occurred around six and yet when Miss Markham arrived the fire had been built up and the channel of the television had been switched to one showing an animated fairy tale—a long one, running for three hours."

"And the dishes had been washed?" Forsythe asked.

"By hand. Mrs. Foster had a dishwashing machine but three cups and saucers, three teaspoons, and two glasses had been washed and neatly set to dry on a dishcloth on the drainboard."

Miss Sanderson's fine brows drew together. "Surely Mrs. Foster might have rinsed the dishes herself."

"No," Chief Inspector Kepesake said. "Prior to the stabbings the Foster family were given massive doses of Seconal. According to Nurse Ines the drug was taken from the cupboard in the doctor's office—"

"When?" Forsythe asked.

Kepesake shrugged. "Before the crimes were committed. Indefinite. The drug was in liquid form, kept for patients unable to swallow pills, and was rarely used."

"Surely that narrows the list of suspects down."

"To patients and friends. In other words to everyone in the village. Dr. Foster was somewhat careless with that cupboard. Would leave people in his office alone and never lock it up. Anyway, as I started to say, it looks as though the drug was put in the teacups and glasses of orange juice. The coroner estimated the children had consumed enough to have killed them. After drinking a powerful dose like that I find it hard to believe Mrs. Foster was capable of gathering up the cups and glasses and washing them."

"I take your point," Forsythe agreed. "You say the doctor's body was mangled?"

"Rather gruesomely. If you like I can show you the official photos."

"Not necessary. But the wife and boys were not?"

"One stab wound in each back. Carefully done, as a medical man might. Looks as though the hate was directed at the doctor, doesn't it?"

"Maybe not, chief," Brummell said. "Could be the other three were stabbed first and by the time the bastard—sorry,

Miss Sanderson. By the time the killer got around to the doctor he just had a taste for blood and ripped and tore."

"Then why didn't he kill the baby girl?" Miss Sanderson asked.

Brummell wiped beer foam from his lips again. "Don't know. Maybe something scared him off. Maybe . . . maybe his lust for blood was satisfied when he mutilated the baby's dad. Hard to say."

She asked another question. "Was the weapon left on the scene?"

"No," Kepesake said. "The police surgeon said the knife blade was long and narrow. Possibly a very sharp butcher knife. The knife didn't come from the Fosters' kitchen."

Leaning forward, Forsythe jabbed at the logs with a poker. The fire blazed up and this time Miss Sanderson, feeling strangely chilled, was glad to feel the surge of heat. They sat quietly, Brummell drinking his beer, Kepesake eyeing the glass case containing pink, white, and green jade, Forsythe tapping a long finger against the arm of his chair. Then Kepesake said rather diffidently, "If you agree to cooperate, Miss Sanderson, we'll give you all the assistance we can. You can visit Miss Sanders' rest home and soak up the family history. I'll give you all our files and photos to study and also a list of the names and descriptions of the villagers. I know you have a remarkable memory."

"Sandy has," Forsythe said. "I can appreciate your position, Kepesake. It does look as though help is needed to loosen the tongues of the locals. But I strongly object to Sandy being staked out like a goat. What about using me? I could pose as a friend of the family—"

"Won't work, old boy. For one thing the newspapers have printed your picture too often. Maddersley-on-Mead may be a bit ingrown and backward but they do get London papers. Besides, how are you going to convince the dead woman's sister, Miss Markham, that you're an old friend?"

"The sister is a suspect?" Miss Sanderson asked.

"A prime suspect. One thing we did discover is that Paul Foster was once Irene Markham's fiancé. Seems she brought him home to meet her pretty young sister and within the month Gillian and Paul were married. Irene was estranged from them until about a year ago. She lived in London and didn't even acknowledge the births of her two nephews. But when Gillian was pregnant with the little girl Irene was persuaded to return to the village. The only person we've located with a motive is Miss Markham."

Without waiting for Forsythe Miss Sanderson reached for the decanter and refreshed her glass. "Who's looking after the baby now?"

"Irene Markham."

"The prime suspect is caring for the only surviving member of the family?"

"I don't like it myself," Kepesake admitted. "But it's only for a short time. The baby's guardian is Dr. Foster's brother. Leonard Foster and his wife are in Saudi Arabia. He's an expert on oil development. They'll be back in England shortly and the child will be given to them. Anyway, if Miss Markham is the murderer I can scarcely see her harming a baby in her care."

"What's the child's name?" Miss Sanderson asked.

"Lucinda," Brummell told her. "Lucinda Gillian Foster, known as little Lucy. A bonny baby, looks like her mother. One thing we haven't mentioned. At the time of her death Mrs. Foster was about three months pregnant."

"Dear God," Miss Sanderson whispered. After a time she glanced up at Forsythe. "Robby, I know you disapprove but I'm going to Maddersley. Mrs. Sutter can take over my work."

"And if I forbid you to go?"

"You'll have my resignation."

Her words dropped like stones into a pool. The silence that followed them rippled out like tiny waves in water. Both Abigail Sanderson and Robert Forsythe were appalled at her threat. More than their professional relationship was at risk. Miss Sanderson was the only mother Forsythe had ever known. He was the boy she'd cherished from child-hood. Above all they were friends.

Adam Kepesake looked embarrassed but Brummell wagged his shaggy head. "Surely," he said gently, "it needn't come to that."

Forsythe moved forward. He took one of his secretary's hands in both of his. Her hand was cold. He squeezed it, trying to warm it. "No," he said. "It certainly won't. Sandy, I'll trust your judgment. But why? The children?"

"The child. It's too late for Arthur or Andrew or for the unborn baby. It's not too late for little Lucy. I have a feel-ing . . ."

"One of your fey feelings again?"

"Perhaps. But I'm needed. When Lucy's guardian claims her, when she's safe, I'll leave that place like a shot. In the meantime . . ."

"In the meantime be careful. Be very careful, Sandy."

TWO

BE VERY CAREFUL, MISS SANDERSON warned herself as she clambered down from the single-decker bus and took her heavy case from the driver. Remember you're now Abigail Sanders, an affluent but frail and aging lady. After the charming letter to Irene Markham that the dying woman had dictated to Miss Sanderson and the way her delicate health had been stressed, it certainly wouldn't do to hop about athletically. Cousin Irene's reply to that letter, although brief to the point of curtness, had acknowledged the need for Miss Sanders' support. A postscript had been added, caustically pointing out it was indeed odd that it had taken a tragedy to bring the two cousins together.

Allowing the case to drag her arm down, Miss Sanderson gazed around the village of Maddersley-on-Mead. The bus had stopped in front of the Fox and Crow and she turned to scrutinize the inn. It wasn't an authentic relic of a long-passed century but rather was a fairly modern structure tarted up with mullioned windows and a brass-bound door. Completely pseudo, she decided, fake beams, imitation leather, and artistically battered pewter, doubtless imported from Japan.

The brass-bound door creaked open and a man strolled
out, bestowed a genial smile on her, and took the case
from her hand. "Paddy Rourke," he told her. "Innkeeper. If
you're looking for accommodations you've come to the
right place. The Fox and Crow is the best in the village.
Also the only. Lunch is being served right now."

She smiled back. "Killarney?"

"County Clare. At least my old dad was from that little
bit of heaven. Does it show?"

"It sounds. The lilt is there."

More than the lilt was there. His milk-white skin, black
curls, and impish blue eyes fairly shrieked Ireland. He was
steering her toward the door but she shook her head.
"Sorry, I won't be staying at the inn. Could you direct me
to the Markham house? I suppose it's called the Foster
house now."

"We still call it the Markham house. You'll be Miss
Sanders then. Come to keep Irene company in her hour of
need. Ah, don't look so surprised. It's a wee place and
news travels fast in Maddersley. I hear you've not been
well. It's a fairish walk and if you'd like to come in and rest
I'll have a delivery van give you a lift to the house."

Miss Sanderson debated. It might be better to walk.
Give her a chance to look the village over. "You're kind,
Mr. Rourke, but my doctor insists on exercise. I'll walk
slowly. But if you could send my case . . ."

"That I'll do. Rog Austin will be making his rounds
about two. Now, as to directions." With his free hand he
pointed up the hill. "The Markham place is on Jericho
Lane. Can't miss it. Church on one corner and Abercrombie's pasture on the other. House is the last one on the
lane. Irene won't be there. Keeps the shop open until five.
But Mrs. Toogood will welcome you."

She thanked him and set off up the walk, shortening her normally loping strides and attempting to look frail. It was a dreary day and sullen clouds banked up in a solid overcast hinted of rain or sleet. Probably sleet. The wind was cold enough to make her turn up her collar and burrow into her heavy coat.

The village looked as dreary as the weather. Past the inn was a greengrocers, a notion shop, and a chemist's. The notion shop was boarded up. On the other side of the street a number of small shops huddled together as though for protection from the chill wind. She checked them mentally against the map Kepesake had showed her. Dora's Tea Shoppe, The Cheese Tease, Marlow's Bakery, Austin's Meat Market, Ferne's General Store. The last shop catered to female clientele. The window was crowded with sweaters, blouses, gloves, and scarves. A gold-lettered sign said merely Irene's. Miss Sanderson wondered whether she should cross over and meet her cousin. She decided against it. Few of the villagers seemed to be braving the October weather. An aged couple tottered out of the meat market and a buxom matron was heading for The Cheese Tease. All of them carried umbrellas.

Beyond the chemist shop was a straggle of row houses, narrow and squalid looking. The last one fell behind and was replaced by a hedged pasture where two cows leaned together under the bare branches of a huge maple. The cobblestoned road trailed off into a gravel surface and curved away toward a stone bridge. The road led to Maddersley Hall, home of the local gentry. That way wasn't for her, at least not yet.

A sign at the corner of the hedge told her she was about to turn onto Jericho Lane. She crossed the narrow road and stopped to examine the church. St. Mark's was on a par with the rest of the village. It was built of gray stone and flint, couldn't decide whether to appear Gothic or Elizabethan and managed to look merely grotesque. The manse, set well back among dark pines, looked like an excellent setting for a horror film. This was the lair of the Reverend Doctor Daniel Clay and his aged housekeeper Mrs. Gay.

The banked clouds, weary of retaining their burden of moisture, decided to release it. Icy sleet pelted down and Miss Sanderson yanked her head scarf closer, drew her long neck turtlelike into the fold of her collar, and resisted an impulse to break into a run. Careful, she warned herself sternly, as Mr. Paddy Rourke had said, this is a wee place and there may be an invisible but avid audience.

Beyond the pine-shrouded manse were three cottages. She gave them an approving look. These were the nicest places she had yet seen. They were identical, neatly fenced, slate-roofed, half-timbered, with small perfectly proportioned windows. They were owned by a gentleman in London and rented to sundry tenants. The first cottage had a bright red door, the next a blue one, and the last a sunshine yellow.

As she neared the first cottage the red door opened and a young woman moved jerkily down two shallow steps. She was modishly dressed in leather—a white coat belted around a narrow waist, black boots reaching high on sparrow legs, and a black leather tam perched jauntily on fair hair that fell lushly to white leather shoulders. In a triangular face huge brown eyes bulged—eyes that didn't need the emphasis of the heavy coating of shadow and black eyeliner that had been painted on.

As Miss Sanderson reached the gate the girl clattered it open and stepped out on the walk. She flashed the older woman a tentative smile and for a moment it looked as though she were about to speak. But the black tam jerked to one side and the girl brushed by. Not as friendly as the innkeeper, Miss Sanderson thought, but then not in a commericial business. Reaching into her splendid memory bank, she brought out the name—Linda Beauchamp, ex-schoolmistress, apprentice writer, ex-patient of Dr. Paul Foster. And, according to Sergeant Brummell, full-time neurotic.

She identified the occupants of the other two cottages. Blue door—Miss Sarah Ines, former hospital nurse and, until recently, devoted aide to the young doctor. The yellow door led onto a shallow wooden ramp. Matthew Johnston—retired carpenter, close friend of the Foster family, a cripple. Taking a deep breath she stopped before the wrought iron gate of the last house on Jericho Lane.

The Markham place was not a cottage but a sprawling two-storied building in plaster and flint. The windows were outlined with dark green shutters, a wide veranda ran the full length of the house and was framed in vines bare now but promising heavenly shade on a hot summer day. A small brass plaque set into the gate announced this was the residence of P. A. Foster, M.D. It was well cared for; the gate didn't creak but swung back silently on well-oiled hinges. Three walks led like spokes in a wheel, one directly to the foot of the veranda, the left one circling around to the back of the house, the right leading along the other side and bearing a white-painted arrow sign lettered *Surgery*.

Sleet stung at her face as she climbed the steps to the shelter of the veranda. On wide boards were bulky objects shrouded in canvas. She pictured wicker furniture awaiting a summons to duty on a drowsy July day. She stepped

onto a mat telling her in green letters that she was welcome, and pressed the bell. Within the recesses of the
house the first bars of the William Tell Overture pealed.
She waited . . . and waited. As her hand reached again for
the bell the door opened a couple of inches revealing a
heavy chain and one small gray eye.

"Well?" Miss Sanderson said impatiently.

The welcome mat appeared to have been lying. The eye
unblinkingly regarded her but no move was made to remove the chain. "Who be you?" a disgruntled voice demanded.

"Abigail Sanders. I'm expected."

"You're late. Thought you'd be here about noon and it's
after one. Figured you'd drive faster than that."

"I don't drive," Miss Sanderson told the eye. She certainly did and would have preferred to have brought her
own sporty car but her namesake couldn't drive and it was
necessary to stay in character. "Are you going to let me in
or not?"

"Hold your horses."

The door thudded closed, the chain rattled, and then it
opened wide and the woman stepped to one side. Miss
Sanderson, chilled, miserable, and now thoroughly annoyed, lunged into the hall. She had time only to note
black-and-white tile, a scarlet telephone on a stand, a staircase that only missed being gracious, and double doors
opening to the left, before the housekeeper began to
speak. "Toogood's the name. Hannah Toogood. You're all
wet. Raining?"

"Sleeting and I'm nearly frozen."

"Be warm enough here. Got central heating. Wish Bert
and me had it. Take off them wet things and get them in

that closet. Don't go tracking up the floor. Just got done scrubbing it."

As Miss Sanderson obeyed she slid glacial eyes over the housekeeper. Mrs. Toogood was a blowsy woman of indeterminate age, clad in a gaudy cotton dress, a voluminous apron, and ancient carpet slippers. Her expression was as disgruntled as her voice. Miss Sanderson had a hunch Hannah Toogood was not going to prove to be one of her favorite people but she must attempt to get along. She held out a small olive branch. "Sorry I was later than expected. Did you hold lunch for me?"

"Don't do meals. Have enough on me hands with the baby and this house. Have to get your own." Mrs. Toogood took off her apron and plucked a gray coat with a ratty rabbit collar from the depths of the closet. "That is if'n you can find any food. Miss Irene don't keep enough food for a sparrow. Now, when the missus was alive it was different. Set a good table did the missus." The woman kicked off her carpet slippers and pushed her feet into rubber boots.

"What are you . . . Mrs. Toogood, are you leaving?"

"My half day. Should have got away sharp at twelve. Gotta take one of the kids—got six little ones, Bert and me—over to the dentist at Lambert. Gonna cost, that dentist acts like he's setting pure gold in them teeth but Edgar, he's our oldest, had me up half the night with the toothache. Not my Bert. Never fear. Swear that man could sleep through anything."

"But you can't leave. The baby. I know *nothing* about babies. The only time I ever see babies are in prams being pushed through parks."

Mrs. Toogood gave her a wide smile. One of her front teeth was missing. "Guess you'll have to learn in a hurry.

If'n you'd got here earlier I'd have been able to show you how." At the panic in the other woman's face the house-keeper relented and patted Miss Sanderson's arm. "No need to take on, Miss Sanders. I just put the little one down and she'll be good for about two hours. Some babies are a trial but not little Lucy. Child's an angel like her mother, rest her soul." She tugged a woolen hat down over untidy mouse-colored hair. "Clothes laid out in the nurs-ery. When she stirs diaper her—"

"Diaper!"

"Nothing to it. These are them disposable nappies. Couldn't afford them for my kids but there's some as can. Bottles made up and in the fridge, her food in the cup-board. Miss Irene will be home after five and take over. Best of luck."

"Wait!" Miss Sanderson wailed as the door started to close. A gray eye peered through the crack. "Clean forgot to tell you. Get that chain on this door and keep it on. Don't let no one in 'less you know them."

"I don't know *anyone*."

"Be awful careful. This is one bad house. Always has been. Someone could come right in and slit your throat!"

Beyond protest Miss Sanderson watched the door thud closed. With a shaking hand she reached for the chain. Nothing, she thought wrathfully, like leaving a person in a strange house where four people had recently been mur-dered and making an exit line like *that*.

THREE

FOR MOMENTS MISS SANDERSON stood glaring at the blank panel of the door. Then she swung around and peered up the shadowy staircase. Somewhere up there little Lucy, blissfully unaware she was now in the hands of a rank amateur, was sleeping. At this point, Miss Sanderson thought, she would rather face that murderous stranger Mrs. Toogood had warned her about than a baby who would have to be diapered and fed.

She gave herself a mental shake. Only minutes into the house and already going to pieces. Perhaps Robby had been right and she should never have come here. At the thought she lifted her chin and squared her thin shoulders. Instead of going into a blue funk she would use the time to look the house over. Again she reached into her memory and drew out the police artist's plan of the house. This wide hall bisected the main floor. Left side devoted to the family's living quarters, right to the doctor's surgery.

Best to get the worst over first. She opened the door into the waiting room. As she stepped onto sand carpeting she noted the door directly opposite. This was the exterior one that opened onto the walk at the side of the house.

The patients had been admitted through it. Crossing the room, she examined the white molding around the door-frame. This was the door by which the police thought the murderer had left. Bloodstains no longer marked the pristine surface. She opened the door and looked down a flight of steep steps. This door, like the front one, locked automatically when the latch clicked. She turned and looked around. The waiting room looked like many she had been in—four imitation leather chairs, a matching couch, plastic-topped tables piled with ancient magazines, in one corner a bank of file cabinets with the nurse's desk in front of them. On the shining desk top there were only two objects. A telephone, brown this time, and a name-plate—Sarah Ines.

At the end of the room was the door to the doctor's office. Remembering the police photos she was far from eager to enter that room. The worst first, she reminded herself, and swung open the door. It looked as ordinary as the waiting room. Someone had done a good job cleaning it up. A wide desk, a swivel chair in back of it, two arm-chairs in front of it, a bank of file cabinets, a bookcase filled with heavy medical books, and the drug cupboard. She wandered over and tried the glass door. Locked. Looking at the empty space that once had contained a bottle of liquid Seconal, she thought nothing like locking the barn door . . .

As she backed away from the cupboard she glanced at the floor area around the desk. The scrubbing hadn't been a success here. Tan carpeting was marred with ugly dark blotches. She closed her eyes, trying to will away the photo of this room, but there it was in dreadful color. Paul Foster's head had rested against the chair back, his face untouched—a handsome man with thick dark hair, wide-set eyes, a good chin. From the throat down, a horror—shirt, vest, pants sliced with powerful strokes, straining away from a mass of protruding intestines—slit like a filleted fish from collarbone to groin. Blood welling onto the desk, the floor, blood spattering the wall. Most dreadful of all—the arms. Lifted onto the desk, one hand touching the open textbook, the other reaching for the tray where a half-smoked cigar lay. Merciful God, Miss Sanderson thought, I hope that drug was powerful. I hope Paul Foster didn't feel that knife shredding his body.

Her eyes snapped open and she saw only dark marks on carpeting. Swinging the last door open, she took a perfunctory look. An examination table, a linen closet, a sink, one straight-backed chair. She made record time returning to the hall.

Where now? The living room, of course. Double doors opened onto a bright cheerful room, salmon and chocolate brown—salmon walls and salmon carpeting, much more luxurious than in the surgery, and brown velour furniture. Two armchairs facing each other across the hearth, gleaming tables, a television set into an expensive rosewood cabinet. On the tabletops the glint of small copper and brass ornaments. Above the mantel was an oil painting of a pastoral scene, not well done but cheerful—white sheep grazing on vivid green turf, lavender hills rising against a cloud-specked sky, a farmhouse perched on a rise, in the foreground two small boys rolling a hoop across improbable green grass.

Small boys. Miss Sanderson looked for and found the children's chairs—a miniature rocking chair with a salmon velour cushion, a small armchair upholstered in chocolate brown. Her mind flashed the scene as it had been that night when Brummell and Adam Kepesake arrived. The

younger boy propped up in the rocker . . . Andrew James
Foster, aged three years, eight months. The older boy in
the armchair . . . Arthur Paul Foster, who hadn't reached
his fifth birthday. Two small boys, quite dead, facing a
television screen on which figures from a fantasy moved
and laughed and sang. On the grate a freshly kindled fire
beaming heat that could never warm those children.

Tears prickled bitterly at her eyes and Miss Sanderson
moved jerkily across the room to the bay window. She
pulled aside salmon-and-brown-striped curtains and looked
across the veranda at lashing sleet. She glimpsed the gate
of the neighboring cottage and leaned forward. A wheelchair was briskly trundling up to the gate. In it crouched a
figure swathed in a heavy coat and tweed cap and a tartan
muffler. A matching tartan rug was tucked around the
man's legs. Matthew Johnston, who once had baby-sat for
his younger neighbors, was returning home. She felt
slightly comforted. If she came to a desperation point with
Lucy she could always run next door for some expert coun-
seling.

She made her way to the dining room. It was rather
small but well appointed—a round cherry table centered
with a bowl of dried flowers, six matching chairs, a towering breakfront sideboard, a silver wine cooler set in a metal
tripod, fine china and glass in the sideboard. She didn't
care for the damask wallpaper or the heavy velvet at the
window but she admitted blowsy Mrs. Toogood was an
excellent housekeeper. Not a speck of dust and the silver
was gleaming. A door opened onto a tiled hall and in a few
paces she reached the swinging door to the kitchen.

Ah, here was a room to be appreciated by lovers of fine
food, and Miss Sanderson, despite her greyhound build,
had a robust appetite. This kitchen was, as all kitchens

should be, the heart of the home. Modern convenience had been marvelously blended with traditional comfort. The wide window was curtained with a checked material and the sill was crowded with red, pink, and white geraniums. A matching checkered cloth covered a large round table. More red-and-white cushioned four ladder-back chairs. Black-and-white tile floored the room and the snowy white squares were echoed in a combination refrigerator and freezer, a dishwashing machine, the metal cupboard doors, and so many small appliances that Miss Sanderson lost count. She cast an approving glance at a long spice rack, patted the wall oven, touched a countertop stove, and realized breakfast was long passed and she was famished. She headed toward the fridge and then pulled up short. Time for her stomach later. Now, back to business.

She returned to the round table and this time deliberately recalled the kitchen photo. Of the four this had been the easiest to take. Gillian Foster, twenty-seven, was seated at the table. Her head had fallen forward and a mass of red-gold hair mercifully masked her face. The ruffled apron Adam Kepesake had mentioned had been tied around her narrow waist. She had looked peaceful and domestic. In front of her a chopping board had been strewn with carrots, tomatoes, celery. In one delicate hand was a paring knife, her other hand lay across the table, slender, shapely, even in death possessing a sense of grace. This time there were no dark splotches. There had been only a small amount of blood and the tile had been wiped clean. Circling the table, Miss Sanderson pulled out a chair. She'd been wrong. Only three chairs had gay cushions. The one Gillian had died on had been removed.

Between the towering refrigerator and the back door was

another door, this one louvered. Behind it was a laundry area containing a clothes-washing machine, a dryer, two deep sinks, and a bank of cupboards above a long counter. The room was bare now but in the police photograph it had been a riot of color. All the party materials had been stored in this room. The dryer had been lost to view under red and blue and yellow balloons, and eight small baskets, heaped with candy, had been lined up near eight party hats. Four were pirate hats for small boys, the rest silver tiaras for equally small girls. On the wall a message cut from red drawing paper and covered with glitter had been tacked. *Happy Birthday, Arthur.*

She found she had been in error when she thought the worst to be faced was in the doctor's office. This room, so festive that night and with no signs of violence, proved to be the hardest to bear. Arthur and Andrew who had been waiting excitedly for the birthday morning, anticipating a party, propped in front of a television and dead, beyond birthdays and parties and life. A wave of rage engulfed her, blurring the contours of the room, knotting her hands into helpless fists. The beast who had wrenched life from those innocent children must be found, must be destroyed.

A bar of the *William Tell* Overture pealed lustily through the house and she jumped. Forgetting Mrs. Toogood's admonitions, she tore off the chain and flung the front door wide. The young man on the veranda looked startled. Behind him, parked half over the curb, was a small gray van lettered in scarlet—*Austin's Meat Market.*

"Rog Austin," he told her. "Paddy from the Fox and Crow asked me to bring this bag up."

She stood aside and he stepped into the hall. For a moment she had thought the innkeeper had decided to bring the case himself. Rog Austin had the Irishman's wiry build and dark curly hair but he was younger, looking barely in his twenties. On closer examination there was little resemblance between the two men. Austin's eyes were that shade of gray that is almost colorless, and he had a fallaway chin, and a full girlish mouth. Miss Sanderson had liked the looks of Rourke but she didn't care at all for Austin's. The colorless eyes were staring avidly around, the full moist lips were parted. He reminded her of the type of person who stops to look at the site of car accidents, hoping to see a mangled body or bloodstains.

His eyes wandered from the closed door to the surgery to the double doors of the lounge. "Miss Markham said as how you aren't well. If you like, Miss Sanders, I can carry your bag up."

"No. The baby is sleeping." Lifting her handbag from the telephone stand she opened it.

He lowered the case and waved the tip away. "Had to make a delivery to Matthew Johnston next door anyway. No problem. Glad to do what I can. Awful thing about those boys, isn't it?"

"To say nothing of their parents."

"Some people ask for what they get, miss. But those kids sure didn't." The restless eyes wandered over her face. "Sure can see you're Miss Markham's cousin. Look something like her. Saw Hannah Toogood getting on the bus with young Edgar and she thought Miss Sanders must be fair nervous 'bout being in this house all alone."

"I fail to see anything to be nervous about, Mr. Austin."

"Rog. Mr. Austin's my dad. Tell you what. No amount of money could keep *me* in this place. Can't figure why Miss Markham didn't stay on in them rooms behind her dress shop."

Miss Sanderson was edging him toward the door. "Kind of you to be concerned and thanks for bringing my case."

"Be careful how you open this door, hear. Make sure you know who's on the other side. Bad place, this house."

"The Fosters, you mean."

"Goes way back beyond that, miss. Back to when this house was built."

Rog Austin had titillated her curiosity but before she could ask a question he was through the doorway and loping down the steps. Fine detective, she lectured herself a golden opportunity to pump that boy and you speed him on his way simply because you don't like his eyes or mouth. She glanced at her watch—after two. She'd better have a look around the first floor before Lucy woke up.

As she mounted the stairs she found she was glad not to have any photographs to recall for these rooms. On the landing she paused to get her bearings. A wide hall led past four closed doors, two to a side, to white painted double doors at the rear. She tried the door to her left—the nursery. Pink walls dotted with blue and silver angels, a white chest and change table, a pink and white crib over which two large ceramic angels hovered protectively. She stepped onto a shaggy white rug and peered down into the crib. Sergeant Brummell had been correct. Lucinda Gillian Foster, aged ten months, was indeed a bonny baby. Red-gold ringlets clustered moistly around a rosy face, coppery lashes rested against plump cheeks, dimpled hands were flung above her head. From one hand a teddy bear dressed in a knit sweater had dropped onto the pillow. A little beauty, Miss Sanderson thought, and tiptoed out, inching the door closed.

Directly across the hall was a large bath with two basins

and much tile. She drew her breath in sharply. On the tile counter two china kittens were perched. Jutting from the heads were toothbrushes. Metal tags dangled from their necks. Arthur on the black kitten, Andrew on the white. Why hadn't these things been removed? Without caring about her hostess' reaction she opened a drawer and thrust the kittens in it.

She took only a glance in the room beside the bathroom. Bunk beds, shelves of toys, two small desks, a row of boy's books, toy trucks lined up in a row on the floor. Beside the nursery she found the guest room. Charming, she decided, spacious, with a double bed, a comfortable armchair and reading light, decorated in primrose and ivory. Rather a lot of ruffles on the spread and curtains. She wondered if this room had been intended for Lucy when the next baby arrived.

Behind the double doors at the end of the hall was the master suite—a huge bedroom, a bath, a dressing room. It was lushly and expensively decorated. The furnishings looked like period pieces, white and gilt and graceful. Her eyes narrowed as she looked around. Every surface was covered with photographs. She picked up one in a silver frame from a bed table and gazed down at the wedding picture of Paul and Gillian Foster. His dark good looks and height accentuated the petiteness of his bride. There was amazing resemblance between mother and daughter. Redgold hair spilled over narrow shoulders, wide eyes smiled, a dimple peeked from a rounded cheek. Putting down the frame, Miss Sanderson looked at the other pictures. On the dressing table was a family group. Paul stood behind his wife's chair, two boys with their father's coloring and wide chin smiled at the camera, Gillian looked fondly down at the baby in her arms, Lucy wore a lacy christening gown.

On the chiffonier was another charming pose of the three children and on the other bed table was a head-and-shoulders-shot of the beautiful Gillian. Miss Sanderson blinked. This obviously was the room Irene Markham was using. How could she bear those faces surrounding her? Why hadn't they been put out of sight? On the dressing table was a silver-backed set of comb and brush and hand mirror with entwined initials—GMF. On the chiffonier was a set of military hairbrushes. She looked in the shallow door of the dressing table and found a tortoise shell comb and brush with Irene's initials. Had the entire suite been left with the murdered couple's possessions still in place?

She checked the bath. There were a huge marble tub with a glass enclosure, double sinks in one counter, the other shaped like an antique dressing table with matching chair. She opened one side of the medicine chest. Ranks of cosmetics and perfumes and nail polishes. In the other were masculine toiletries and two electric razors.

"Blimey," she whispered and walked into the dressing room fully expecting to be faced with rows of Gillian and Paul Foster's clothes. But the long rods were virtually empty. Only three women's suits, a trouser suit, several dresses, and a tailored robe huddled at the end of one. On the shoe rack were two pair of walking shoes, a pair of leather slippers, and one pair of black pumps. She instinctively knew these clothes had not belonged to the lovely Gillian.

At the head of the stairs she paused and considered. Thus far her tour of the house had only disclosed three facts. The Fosters had lived well, surrounded by all modern conveniences and expensive fittings. The couple had doted on their children. Irene Markham, who once had expected to marry Paul Foster, wasn't squeamish about living with their pictures and intimate possessions.

Not an impressive list. Perhaps after she had a good meal her mind would hum along at a better pace.

The good meal, much to Miss Sanderson's dismay, didn't materialize. In the wonderful kitchen with all its promise and appliances the cupboards were close to bare. Aside from bottles for the baby and a plentitude of milk the huge refrigerator contained only a chunk of moldy cheese. A search of the cupboards revealed rows of tins and jars of baby food and a lone tin of peach halves. The bread box yielded half a loaf of stale bread. There didn't appear to be any butter to put on it.

Miss Sanderson decided to console her groaning stomach with a strong cup of tea. It wasn't brewed when a whimper, followed by a lusty bellow, alerted her to the fact she was to be denied even that small solace.

Swearing under her breath, she headed toward little Lucy's room.

FOUR

LATE AFTERNOON FOUND MISS SANDERSON seated at the kitchen table wearily sipping the tea she had promised herself nearly two hours before. In desperation she was dipping baby biscuits and inelegantly gobbling them.

"When Aunt Irene gets here," she promised the baby, "I'm going to give her a large piece of my mind. Fine welcome for a long-lost cousin who supposedly hauls herself from a sickbed to render assistance. No food, an empty house, and a baby!" Lucy hauled herself up the bars of the playpen and gave Miss Sanderson an enchanting smile, displaying two teeth and a deep dimple. Miss Sanderson couldn't help smiling back. "I take that back about the baby. Mrs. Toogood was right, Lucy, you're an angel."

The angel tolerantly had allowed herself to be picked out of bed, stripped down, washed, powdered, and, after trial and error and fumbling, swathed in nappies and fluffy pink coveralls. Before that had been accomplished Miss Sanderson's brow was dewed with perspiration, but Lucy had cooed, smiled, blown bubbles, and come willingly into a stranger's arms.

In the kitchen Miss Sanderson moved the walnut high

chair out from the wall and spread food on the table. She spooned into the baby's eager mouth dreadful looking pureed spinach, banana custard, and then gave her a bottle of formula. The process was a messy one and when Miss Sanderson turned her back the angel, with a crow of delight, added to the mess by dumping a bowl on the floor.

"Don't waste food," Miss Sanderson scolded. "Heavens knows in this house it's a precious commodity."

After the child was deposited in the playpen Miss Sanderson collapsed at the table and proceeded to fill an ashtray with partially smoked cigarettes and ashes. She didn't smoke much but Cousin Abigail Sanders had admitted that during days of better health she had been a heavy smoker. "Although Gillian and Irene never knew me," the sick woman had warned her stand-in, "some word about me might have filtered back to them. To be on the safe side remember you don't drive, do smoke a great deal, and enjoy an occasional scotch and soda."

Miss Sanderson told the baby. "Right now I'd enjoy a scotch and soda and a steak three inches thick." She cocked her head and listened. "Ah, think I hear your aunt, no doubt bearing ingredients for a large and delicious dinner."

A key grated in the lock, the knob turned, and Irene Markham, dressed as though she'd just returned from an expedition to Antartica, stepped in. A knitted hat was pulled down over her eyes, the collar of a wet anorak was pulled up to her ears, and, to her hungry guest's dismay, she carried only a handbag and an umbrella. Kicking off dripping boots onto Mrs. Toogood's freshly washed tile, she advanced with a mittened hand extended. "Abigail," she said in a high, light voice. "We finally meet. Rather odd, isn't it?"

"Distinctly odd," Miss Sanderson said, touching the wet woolen mitt gingerly. Could that delicious dinner be stuck in the anorak's bulging pockets?

Irene glanced down at her hands and hastily pulled off the mitts. "I feel so awkward, not knowing whether to embrace you or . . ." She looked around. "Where's Mrs. Toogood?"

"Gone."

"That dratted woman! I asked her to stay until I got home. To keep you company and see you got a good rest after your trip. When did she leave?"

"About one. She bolted as soon as I arrived."

"Oh no," the other woman wailed. "Lucy! How did you manage? Do you know anything about—"

"Hadn't the foggiest but I muddled through."

Pulling off the hat, Irene smoothed down her short brown hair, and zipped down the anorak. "Well, at least you had a decent lunch."

"A bit difficult to make a decent lunch from moldy cheese and stale bread."

Irene marched to the fridge and threw open the door. "She didn't even do *that*. She was told to ring up and have an order delivered. That—" The other woman proceeded to give a detailed opinion of her housekeeper. Miss Sanderson's mouth dropped open. Irene Markham had swearing down to a fine art. She questioned Mrs. Toogood's parentage, the possibility her mother had belonged to the canine race, her life-style, and some rather unusual sexual habits. Finally she ran out of curses and sagged back against the white enamel door. "The shops are closed and it's too late to get anything. Well, there just has to be something in the freezer." Opening the other door, she pulled out a frosty package, looked at it, and threw it on the counter. "Fish fingers and chips. Oh, my God!"

She burst into tears and buried her face in her hands. Forgetting her own problems, Miss Sanderson put her arms around the damp anorak and heaving shoulders. "There, there. It's not as bad as all that. We'll manage." She nudged the other woman over to a chair and gently pushed her down on it. "We could both use a drink. Do you have anything?"

"Dining room," Irene sobbed.

"Get that wet coat off."

In the sideboard she found a supply of wines and spirits. Selecting a bottle of single malt, she poured two large drinks with a dribble of soda. When she carried the glasses into the kitchen she found Irene had regained her composure. Her coat was hung on a peg near the door, she'd neatened her hair, and was scrubbing her face off with a damp towel. Taking the drink, she blurted, "I don't know what you think of me, Abigail. Going to pieces like that. I'm at my wit's end. It was only two weeks ago I came in here and found . . . them. It's been a nightmare. Hellish!"

"I know. That's why I'm here. You relax and I'll get supper on. There's a tin of peaches for dessert and some tomato sauce to go with the chips."

The baby threw a stuffed toy out of the playpen and Miss Sanderson gave her a biscuit. The child cooed and started to gnaw at it. "Good baby."

"And Mrs. Toogood *is* good with her. As she tells anyone who'll listen, the only reason she stays on here is because of her dead missus' memory and little Lucy. She was devoted to Gillian."

Miss Sanderson turned on the oven and located a shallow pan. "She seems a fine housekeeper, too."

"To have satisfied my sister she would have to be. But now Mrs. Toogood does exactly as she wishes. We don't get along and the only reason I keep *her* on is because I simply can't find anyone else willing to work here."

"She did mention it's a bad house. And Rog Austin, when he brought my case up, said it's been since it was built. Any idea what the boy was talking about?"

"Village rumors and superstition."

"Nothing factual?"

"If you don't mind I'd rather not discuss things like that now. I know you're anxious to hear about Gillian and the boys but perhaps later?"

"No rush," Miss Sanderson told her falsely. There was a rush. Until she got some details she was at sea.

While she got the scanty supper Irene polished off her drink and went to the dining room for the bottle. She held it up invitingly but Miss Sanderson shook her head. "Maybe after supper."

Pouring a hefty amount, Irene told her, "I'm drinking too much. Funny, before this all happened I barely touched the stuff but now I'm reaching for the bottle far too often."

Go right ahead, Miss Sanderson told her silently as she served the fish fingers and chips. Alcohol loosens tongues. While they ate she shot sidelong looks at her supposed cousin. Irene Markham bore a striking resemblance to the genuine cousin, Abigail Sanders. She had the sick woman's fine features, the same fine texture of hair, the same milky blue eyes. Irene was much the younger. Miss Sanderson couldn't see much resemblance to herself. Chief Inspector Kepesake had been correct. There was only a superficial resemblance. Height, build, coloring. Her own nose was longer, her chin stronger, her eyes larger and a pale clear blue.

Scooping up the last shred of peach, Irene said, "That wasn't bad. I promise you an abundance of food tomorrow. In the morning I'll phone the shops and have Rog Austin bring the other supplies with the meat order. Any preferences?"

"I was wondering. While I'm here would you like me to shop and cook dinner?"

Milky blue eyes fastened on the older woman's face. "I hardly expected you to be able to cook. I mean your parents were so much better off than mine and you probably had servants."

Miss Sanderson opened her mouth to answer and then hesitated. She'd been about to blurt out the truth, that her aunt Rose had insisted she learn to cook. She'd better watch her tongue. She said carefully, "Mother thought a girl should know her way around the kitchen. I'm rather a good cook."

"Did Aunt Grace teach you?"

Not knowing whether Aunt Grace had been a good cook or not Miss Sanderson decided on the truth. "Our cook Aggie took care of lessons. She's a bit of a tyrant." And was still being a tyrant. She'd inherited Aggie from her aunt and right at present the cook was impatiently awaiting Miss Sanderson's return to the flat Aggie ruled with a mailed fist.

"It must have been nice," Irene told her enviously, "having oodles of money and servants and going to the best schools. My parents had quite a struggle."

Miss Sanderson cast an ironic glance around the dream kitchen. "It doesn't look as though you really suffered much."

"Oh, this." Irene waved a hand. "Gillian and Paul had the entire house done over shortly after their marriage. Converted the drawing room and den into the surgery and had central heating installed and new bathrooms put in. Believe me, during my parents' time it wasn't like this. I've always loved this house. Never forgiven father for willing it to Gillian. Strange how this family runs to trouble between sisters. Gillian and me. Your mother and mine." Her eyes coldly examined Miss Sanderson's borrowed brooch and earrings. "I see you're wearing grandmother's amethysts."

"They're not valuable, Irene. I've always considered a few trinkets were a silly reason for our mothers' estrangement."

"There's such a thing as sentimental value," Irene snapped. "And it was more than the amethysts and that gold locket and the rings. Grandmother left Aunt Grace her china and silver too. Mother never forgave her sister. She thought Aunt Grace should have shared the family heirlooms with her."

Miss Sanderson said mildly, "All this happened before either of us were born."

"It wasn't only the inheritance. There was more to it than that."

Having been filled in on the family history, Miss Sanderson asked, "Husbands, you mean?"

"Your father was my mother's suitor until he met Aunt Grace. Mother had to settle for an estate agent and your mother married a factory owner."

"Somewhat similar to the breach between you and Gillian."

Irene had been becoming quite heated but now she settled back in her chair and took a sip of whiskey. "History does tend to repeat itself. But the trouble between Gillian and me began long before she took Paul away from me. Mother had difficulty bearing children, you know—" She stopped abruptly. "How foolish of me. Of course you don't know. Anyway, there were seven years between Gillian and me. By the time she came along mother was in her forties and had given up hope of having a second child. Mother always called my sister 'her miracle baby' and father called her 'his little princess.'" Irene turned and looked down at her tiny niece who was hugging a stuffed lamb. "Lucy's the picture of my sister at the same age. Neither mother nor father were good-looking people and they were overwhelmed by Gillian's beauty. They doted on the child. From the moment of her birth I was pushed aside. Irene was only Gillian's plain gawky sister."

"It must have been difficult to adjust."

"Impossible. Comparisons were constantly made, not only by my parents but by everyone. Gillian's hair and eyes and dimples. I felt like the ugly stepsister."

"This house was left to your sister?"

"Everything was hers. Every cent my parents could scrimp and save was set aside for her. I was given a business education and as father told me years ago, I was competent to make my own way in life but Gillian wasn't and had to be looked after." Irene bowed her head. Her neck looked long and incredibly fragile. "And then I was fool enough to bring the only man I'd ever loved here to meet her."

"Why did you do it?"

"A good question." Irene lifted her head and shook fine brown hair away from her thin face. "One that often occurs to me. I suppose I felt sure of him, secure. I was so proud of Paul. His family were quite poor but a godfather had provided funds for his education and he was educated at Rugby and New College at Oxford. When we met he had just finished his training at Guy's Hospital. We were planning on marrying as soon as he set up practice. Paul asked to meet my family and there were only Gillian and you and, of course, you didn't count."

"Thanks," Miss Sanderson said coldly, thinking of the gentle courageous woman she was impersonating.

"Abigail, I am so *sorry*. That was rude, wasn't it? But how could I take my fiancé around to meet a cousin I'd never met? Anyway, Paul and I came here. Gillian and Paul took one look at each other and a month later sneaked off to London and were married."

"You were estranged from them for a time?"

"For nearly five years. I went back to London and buried myself in my work. Gillian sent birth announcements for Andrew and Arthur but I ignored them. Then Paul came to see me. Gillian was pregnant again and not well and he begged me to return to Maddersley for her sake. He wanted me to live with them, to be as he said 'a part of their family.'"

"And you came back."

"Again I wonder why. Perhaps it was to be near Paul. Perhaps it was because I was lonely. I've never made friends easily and in London all I had was my work, a tiny flat, a few acquaintances. So I agreed to come back to the village but I refused to live in this house with them. I had some savings so I rented my shop and started a little business in ladies' apparel." She gave a rueful laugh. "Not terribly profitable but I manage to get by and there are a couple of small rooms at the rear of the building that I fixed up as living quarters." Irene stretched out a hand for the scotch bottle as the baby threw the lamb out of the playpen and wrinkled up her face as though about to start howling.

"Shouldn't Lucy be in bed?" Miss Sanderson asked.

"Look at the time!" Irene jumped up. "I'll tuck her in and tidy up the kitchen. You can wait in the living room."

Miss Sanderson scooped the child up. "I'll take care of her."

"Do you think you can? She'll need a bottle and—"

"I'm practically a professional now. Had lots of practice this afternoon and I'm a quick study."

There's really nothing to this baby stuff, Miss Sanderson decided happily as she washed, oiled, powdered, and adjusted nappies neatly. She sang to the baby as she snapped up powder-blue sleepers and Lucy responded by blowing bubbles. Tucking the baby into the crib, she pulled up the comforter, snugged the teddy bear in beside the warm body, and handed a bottle to the little one. Nothing to it, she thought as she jauntily blew a kiss and snapped off the overhead light. Beside the crib a night-light cast a rosy glow over the hovering angels. "Take good care of her," she told them and closed the door.

In the downstairs hall a rectangle of light fell from double doors across the tile. Stepping into the living room, she found Irene Markham had made good use of the time. A fire was burning briskly and a gateleg table had been pulled over between the armchairs flanking the hearth. The scotch bottle, glasses, an ice bucket, and soda sat on the gleaming tabletop. Irene, she was pleased to note, had filled her glass and, from the liquid's deep amber color, hadn't paid much attention to the soda.

"Do help yourself," Irene said.

Miss Sanderson made a weak drink and scrutinized her companion. The single malt was doing its job. Color man-

tled Irene's cheeks and her thin lips looked looser. Good,
now for some alcoholic confidences. "Irene, I feel so . . .
so at sea. Gillian is only a name to me. What was she
like?"

"Oodles of pictures upstairs. She loved having her picture taken. I'll get them and you can see for yourself."

"Don't bother. I don't mean what she looked like. I'm
sure she must have been lovely judging by her daughter.
But what was she actually *like*?"

"She was an eighteen-carat bitch-on-wheels."

"Do you really mean that?"

"No. That's spite and jealousy talking. What was Gillian
like?" Irene leaned her head back against brown velour and
for a moment the older woman thought she'd passed out.
But then she said softly, "Many people liked her. Some
loved her. Gillian was possibly the most dangerous woman
I've ever known."

"Was she conceited? A troublemaker? Promiscuous?"

"God, no! She was sweet and rather gentle. She devoted
every minute, every bit of strength to her children and her
husband and her home. After her marriage she never
looked at another man. She tried to be kind to her neighbors and the other villagers."

"And she was dangerous?"

"In a strange way—by trying to be *too* kind and good,
by thirsting to be liked and admired."

"Most people want to be liked and admired."

"Not as passionately as my sister did." Irene stretched
long legs toward the hearth. "I doubt I can make you understand."

"Try."

"Gillian tried to give everyone what he or she wanted
from her. For example, take our parents. She had each of

them convinced she loved them best. Mother believed Gillian loved her more than father and father was convinced his little princess cared most for him. In a way she drove a wedge between them. It extended far beyond family. Another example is Mrs. Toogood. She worshipped my sister and yet if Gillian had decided she wanted another housekeeper, Mrs. Toogood would have been sent packing. Abigail, it's a dangerous game to toy with people's emotions."

"I take it Gillian's emotions didn't run deep."

"Completely superficial."

On the last word Irene slurred and Miss Sanderson hastened to milk more information from her. "Did these shallow emotions include her children and husband?"

"Not her children. Gillian was devoted to them, considered them extensions of herself. Paul? I don't believe she genuinely loved him. When she saw him she wanted him but perhaps it was because he was handsome and a professional man. A man who would make a wonderful father for her wonderful children."

"Before Paul. Were there men in her life?"

"Any number."

"Did she have them convinced she reciprocated their affection?"

"Absolub . . . ab-so-lute-ly." Irene chuckled. "Methinks I'm getting a little tiddly."

Methinks you're getting a little sloshed, Miss Sanderson told her silently. Aloud she asked, "Who?"

Irene was looking owlishly at her—one eye closed—and Miss Sanderson thought it was a wink. "See two Abigails. You see two Irenes?"

Well, Miss Sanderson thought resignedly, what can I

expect? Irene's put a huge hole in that bottle. "Did these men think your sister loved them?"

"Led them right down the garden pash . . . path. Shocked . . . you wouldn't believe when dear little Gillian married." Irene tilted slightly and pushed herself up. She swayed. "Gotta get to bed. Warm bed for Paul and Gillian. Cold for poor gawky Irene. Where in hell's the door gone?"

Even with Miss Sanderson's help the trip to the hall was an erratic one. Loath to give up, she asked, "Why do the villagers think this house is bad? What happened here?"

"Murders."

"You mean the Fosters."

"More'n that." The woman listed slightly to the left and grasped at the newel post. "Not to worry your little head. Doors and windows all locked tight." She hauled herself up the stairs. On the landing she made a laborious about-face and peered down the stairwell. Her face was in shadow but her voice was loud and clear. "Nothing *bad* in this house. Comes from outside. With *knives*."

She lurched out of sight and Miss Sanderson stood as though turned to stone. Mrs. Toogood wasn't the only one with great exit lines. Resisting a strong desire to bolt up the stairs, she forced herself to return to the living room. She banked the fire, carried the bottles back to the sideboard, and took the glasses to the kitchen. Depositing the glasses in the dishwashing machine she stepped over to the windows and hastily yanked the gay curtains over the dark glass.

From outside, she thought, and with knives.

FIVE

BY THE TIME MISS SANDERSON left the Markham house the sun was directly overhead and lemony light streamed down over the village. The wind was still brisk and she was glad of her heavy coat, muffler, and sturdy boots. She strode along Jericho Lane and had reached the church at the corner before she recalled her delicate health. As she shortened her steps she thought of the morning just past. By the time she'd crawled out of bed Irene Markham had left for her shop. The woman had a number of excellent reasons for loathing the Fosters but were her feelings strong enough to kill?

As for Mrs. Toogood, Miss Sanderson found her initial distaste for the woman waning. Granted, the housekeeper's manner hadn't improved from the previous day and she'd appeared delighted to mention there wasn't a "crumb" in the house for lunch. To add to Miss Sanderson's misery she'd pointed out a bulging brown paper bag containing her own lunch. But at the same time she had been spooning gruel into Lucy's eager mouth with every evidence of a tenderness of which Miss Sanderson, Lucy's ardent admirer, strongly approved.

Hitching her shoulder bag up and swinging a string shopping bag, Miss Sanderson strolled down past Abercrombie's pasture and the decrepit row houses. Mrs. Toogood had confided that she and her Bert and the kids lived in the one beside the chemist's shop. It looked like a suitable home for her. As Miss Sanderson crossed the street toward the row of shops she saw the buxom matron she had noticed the previous afternoon marching down the walk. The woman looked stonily at a point past Miss Sanderson's left shoulder but did jerk her head. Let's hope, the secretary-turned-sleuth thought, the merchants prove friendlier than the pedestrians.

Conscious of her empty stomach she made a beeline for Dora's Tea Shoppe. Dora, despite the fact that it was the lunch hour, wasn't doing a roaring business. An elderly couple hunched over a pot of tea in one corner and they comprised the entire clientele. The decor was no more reassuring. A combination of lavender wallpaper and lilac paint had been used with disastrous results. The tables were covered with lavender linen and the rattan chairs looked hideously uncomfortable. Selecting the window table, Miss Sanderson sank on a chair and found her hunch had been correct. She picked up a menu encased in lilac plastic and winced—creamed peas on toast, creamed tuna on toast, creamed sweetbreads on toast. Ugh!

Swinging doors opened and a woman looking somewhat like a large sheep draped in lilac print bustled out. A grimace that might have been a smile twitched up long lips. She extended a gracious hand. "How nice that you've dropped in, Miss Sanders. I saw you yesterday when you arrived and I thought, Dora, that poor dear looks exhausted. I was glad to see Paddy Rourke take your bag. It looked frightfully heavy." Miss Sanderson accepted the hand and found hers not only wrung vigorously but retained in Dora's moist clasp. "Now, you must call me Dora. We don't stand on formality in this little place. You're . . ."

"Abigail."

"Of course. Irene Markham mentioned your name. We're all so glad you came to her aid. Such a horrid business and dear Irene has aged since it happened. But we mustn't spoil your nice lunch talking about that. You will be wanting lunch?"

"Yes." Miss Sanderson managed to extricate her hand from the woman's clasp. "I notice you have a special."

"Have a special every day. Takes work and I don't keep a girl on in the winter—not enough business, you see. Today's is a nice shrimp and veggie plate."

Sounds more promising than creamed toast, Miss Sanderson thought. "I'll have the special."

"Good choice. You'll like it." Small eyes wandered to the window and Dora leaned forward to twitch a lilac curtain aside. The buxom matron was just pushing through the door of the Fox and Crow. "That Nettie Seton! How ladies can stand greasy grill food I can't fathom. Shows too. Nettie's much too heavy and her skin's deplorably oily. I pride myself on no grill and no grease. Well, never mind. Nettie will see the error of her ways. I'll get your luncheon. Only be a jiff. I'll bring you tea."

Miss Sanderson enviously eyed the wide door of the inn. Behind that door was lovely greasy grill food. She pictured crisp bacon, links of sausage, kidneys . . . In a swirl of lilac print the tea was delivered and it was excellent, hot and dark. The china was also nice, blue-and-white willowware. The lunch, when it arrived, was more deplorable than Nettie Seton's oily skin. Stifling a groan, she stared down at a few unidentifiable pink objects swimming in a white paste—on toast, of course. An anemic slice of tomato and a drooping leaf of lettuce completed that day's special.

Dora told her jovially, "Now that won't expand your waistline, Abigail."

It certainly won't, Miss Sanderson thought. If I was starving I still couldn't eat this goo. How on earth did Dora maintain her own generous figure? Could she be a closet patron of the Fox and Crow?

The elderly couple had drained their teapot and were pulling on coats and adjusting scarves. They passed Miss Sanderson's table and flashed smiles at her. She smiled back and watched them totter out. On the walk they paused to speak to a heavy-set woman dressed in shapeless tweeds and heavy brogues. An equally shapeless felt hat drooped over the woman's face and she clasped a sturdy blackthorn cane. From the way the old people were practically bowing and scraping this woman must be a figure of some importance in the village. She soon proved this. Banging open the door she entered the shop, bringing with her a gust of cold air and an aura of command.

"Dora," she bellowed. "Where in tarnation are you? I'm starved."

That makes two of us, Miss Sanderson thought. Dora bolted from the kitchen. She snatched a menu from a table. "You won't be long. The special—"

"Blast your special. I've been taking a tramp on the moors and I'm hungry. I want *food*. Got any sausage?"

"Alfred didn't make any up this morning."

"What *have* you got?"

"Boiled beef, the way you like it."

"That'll have to do. Fry up a heap of potatoes and make

sure the mustard is hot." Without lowering her voice, the
newcomer brayed, "Dora, have you forgotten your man-
ners? Introduce us."

Miss Sanderson thought the woman hadn't noticed her
but the blackthorn was poking in her direction. Dora,
practically simpering, hastened to comply. "This is Miss
Mary Maddersley of Maddersley Hall. Her brother is—"

"I'm well aware who my brother is." The cane struck the
floor sharply. "For God's sake, Dora, stop babbling and tell
me *her* name."

"Abigail Sanders," Miss Sanderson said crisply. "Irene
Markham's cousin and—"

"The long-lost cousin, eh? Got the Markham build and
height. Don't have their nose or chin or eyes." Without
waiting for an invitation she thumped down on a chair,
unbuttoned her jacket, and propped the cane against the
table. She gave Miss Sanderson's plate a disgusted look.
"You're not planning to eat that goop, are you?"

"I don't think I can."

"Dora! Get that garbage out of here and make that two
orders of beef. Hop to it."

As the plate was whisked away, Miss Sanderson
breathed a sigh of relief. "Thanks. You saved my life, to
say nothing of my stomach."

"Got to assert yourself. Dora's a fair cook but she's got
the insane notion ladies shouldn't eat anything unless it's
dripping with mucilage. Hmm, you look much healthier
than I figured you would."

Conscious of the shrewdness of the eyes in the strong-
featured face, Miss Sanderson said, "Since I arrived in
Maddersley I do feel better. Must be the country air."

"If it works that fast we should bottle it." Her companion fished in a handbag and extracted a package of small cigars. "Care for one?"

Shaking her head, Miss Sanderson produced her cigarettes and they proceeded to smoke in what appeared to be a companionable silence. She decided she liked the other woman. Miss Mary Maddersley, chatelaine of Maddersley Hall and only sister of Sir Donald Maddersley, struck her as her own type of person. And she certainly could handle the overly genteel Dora. She wondered how to edge the conversation in the direction she desired. With this formidable grande dame she had a feeling she would get straight answers. As it worked out there was no necessity to verbally maneuver Miss Maddersley. The other woman puffed out a cloud of aromatic smoke and confided, "Shouldn't be smoking. Shouldn't drink either. Blood pressure. Dr. Foster warned me repeatedly cigars and whiskey could finish me off. Told him at least I would die happy. Good doctor, young Foster, but he certainly had a taste for the lassies—"

"Really, Miss Maddersley!" With trembling hands Dora lowered hot platters in front of them. Lowering her voice, she whispered, "If Ernie hears you've talked about his daughter with Abigail . . . well, you know how violent he can get."

"Balderdash! Ernie Marlow doesn't scare me. Shouldn't bother you either." Grabbing the knob of her cane, she flourished it. "Now, you get back to your kitchen and no eavesdropping."

Despite her interest in the lasses and Paul Foster, Miss Sanderson was devouring her meal. She had a feeling it wasn't wise to prod Miss Maddersley. The other woman cut up her beef, dabbed mustard on it, and proceeded to talk. "Must admit I didn't tell the police much about the Fosters. Didn't take to the chief inspector who interviewed Donnie and me. Looked like a tailor's dummy." Miss Sanderson bent her head to hide a grin. That was her own favorite description of Adam Kepesake. "But I don't mind talking to you and, to tell you the truth, I want to see whoever did that put away. Can't say I was fond of the Fosters but no one should die that way, particularly children. How's the baby?"

"Flourishing. Lucy's a lovely child."

"Takes after her mother. Though where Gillian got those looks from is anyone's guess. Emma and Roger Markham were people you wouldn't look twice at. Irene's plain too. Always felt sorry for Irene. Must have been harrowing having a little sister who looked like Gillian."

Miss Sanderson steered the conversation back to Paul Foster and his lasses. "I fail to understand how a man could be interested in other women with a beautiful wife like Gillian."

"That isn't hard to figure out." Dabbing mustard from her lips with lavender linen, Miss Maddersley chuckled. "Like caviar and champagne, have them everyday and you get a longing for mince and beer. Now, I'm not saying Paul Foster cheated on his wife and I'm not saying he didn't. But there was Melanie Marlow and that Beauchamp woman. No one can tell me Melanie was hustled out of the village by the Fosters just because her father was giving her a few licks. From what I saw of that miss she *needed* a good belting. No siree, Gillian wanted her out of the house. Melanie was only sixteen, pretty as a picture, and wild as they come. Probably set her cap for the doctor. But I will tell you this. The Fosters not only made enemies of the Marlows but had Nell Austin ready to kill them."

"Austin's Meat Market?"

"Rog's mother. Now, there's a virago. Too bad Ernie and Nell Austin hadn't teamed up. She'd have been a match for him. But people are always drawn toward their opposites and Maybelle Marlow and Alfred Austin are both rabbits."

"But why would Nell Austin care about Melanie Marlow?"

"Rog, that's why. Nell had her heart set on making a match between her son and the baker's daughter. Nell and Ernie Marlow planned on the marriage from the time the young ones were babes in arms."

"Were Rog and Melanie agreeable?"

"Rog couldn't wait to marry the girl but Melanie couldn't see him for dust. Has a lot more spirit than her mother ever did. Maybelle's always has been like Dora's lettuce— wilted." Setting down her cup, Miss Maddersley leaned across the table. "You're drinking this in. I'm glad we met. Had me puzzled why the sudden interest in a group of relatives you had never met. I've a hunch I've the answer now."

Miss Sanderson struggled to look puzzled. This woman's intelligence could well not only unmask her but put an end to her sleuthing. "I think any person would be outraged at having relatives killed the way the Fosters were."

"I agree." Miss Maddersley lowered her voice. "I sense things. Always have. My grandmother was born with a caul and she did too. I sense you are not what you seem. Are you connected with the police?"

"No."

The other woman gnawed her lip thoughtfully. "I don't feel you're lying. Let me put it another way. Are you here to uncover the fiend who killed those children?"

Miss Sanderson debated. Then she threw caution to the winds. "Yes."

"Thought you were. No way the villagers will open up to the police. Inbred bunch and I'm no better. Didn't tell that stuffed shirt Kepesake anything. But I like you and I admire your style. As I said before, the murderer must be unmasked. God knows what he'll do next."

"Miss Maddersley, do you think Lucy Foster is in danger?"

"Hard to say. My guess is she isn't."

"But the rest of her family—"

"True. But if the baby was on the murderer's list she would have been killed that night. I think Gillian or Paul or perhaps both of them were the targets. The boys were killed simply because they were witnesses and quite old enough to give the name. Lucy wasn't and so she was left unharmed. Make sense?"

"It does."

"You come to the Hall tomorrow. I'll tell you what I know. Mind you, it's rumors and conjecture—"

"I'd be grateful."

"Make it around four. We'll have tea. Donnie won't be home then."

She buttoned up her jacket, threw some money on the table, and retrieved her cane. Without a backward glance she strode out of the tearoom. Dora popped out from behind the kitchen door as though she had been stationed there. Miss Sanderson had been wondering how this woman felt about Mary Maddersley, whether she resented the woman's brusque treatment. Dora's words bore out not only her resentment but also the fact she had been eavesdropping. "Fine one she is to talk about the Marlows and Austins! Don't believe a word she said about them, Abigail.

If anyone in this village had a grudge against Gillian and the doctor it's that brother of hers!" She added venomously, "And him not right in the head either."

Miss Sanderson had had enough of the tearoom and of Dora. She had no desire to listen to the woman and liked her no better than she had her creamed shrimp. As she paid for her lunch she found it an effort to be civil. Dora charged her double, for the untouched special as well as for the beef. She added a tip and the sheep face beamed. "Didn't hear all she had to say, Abigail. Started to whisper."

And I'm grateful she did, Miss Sanderson thought. She told the woman, "Miss Maddersley invited me to tea tomorrow. Lovely person."

Dora looked thunderstruck. "Oh, she is, she most certainly is. A valued patron and a valued friend. I do trust, Abigail, you won't mention what I just said. Nerves, you know, we've all been so nervy since the dear Fosters died."

Miss Sanderson contented herself with a noncommittal smile. Let two-faced Dora simmer in her own foul sauces. But, as she admitted, she couldn't afford to be so selective of informants. She had a tendency to shy away from the ones she didn't like.

She headed toward The Cheese Tease, vowing that even if she loathed the proprietor she would dig for all the gossip she could.

SIX

WHEN MISS SANDERSON BEGAN the return journey to the
Markham house her arm was weighed down by the pur-
chases in the string bag. But except for the time spent in
Dora's Tea Shoppe her efforts had been wasted. The
Cheese Tease, as its name implied, did specialize in a wide
assortment of that delicacy and also featured homemade
preserves, small crocks of honey, and exotic blends of tea.
It was run by a mother-daughter team. The daughter had
bright blue eyes and soft brown hair. The mother had soft
brown eyes and bright blue hair. Both women were pleasant and extended Miss Sanderson a warm welcome to the
village but weren't given to gossip. All she had acquired in
their shop were remarks on the weather, a fine piece of
Stilton, and a jar of ginger jam.

Her visits to the butcher shop and the bakery hadn't
been any more productive. Alfred Austin proved to be a
short man with a narrow chest and a paunch that belled
out his stained apron. He had the round pink face of a
cherub and a hairless skull. His wife Nell, the virago, was
several inches taller than her husband and displayed icy
civility to their new customer. There was a marked re-

semblance between Nell and her son. Both had curly dark hair and colorless eyes. But Nell didn't have loose lips and a fall-away chin. Her mouth was as tight as a rattrap and her chin jutted like a rock. While Alfred and his wife made up the order Rog wandered in from the rear of the shop. He greeted Miss Sanderson like an old friend and promised to bring her order on the first delivery. Rog was evidently the apple of the maternal eye. When Nell looked at him her rattrap mouth softened. Alfred seemed to be busy avoiding looking at either his wife or son. Miss Sanderson thought the little man hardly fulfilled the popular image of a brawny butcher.

In the bakery shop next door she found a man who *did* look like a butcher. Ernie Marlow was huge and reminded her vividly of Boris Karloff. Above gigantic shoulders was a huge head, brutish features, a shock of coarse hair. Yet, as he arranged pastries on a long tray, his enormous hands moved with an odd delicacy. His wife, as Mary Maddersley had remarked, was his direct opposite. Maybelle was short, curvaceous, with a softly pretty face. She was heavily made up but the powder and rouge didn't quite conceal a fading bruise under one eye. She was much younger than her hulking husband. Miss Sanderson tried to entice the couple into conversation but Ernie ignored her and Maybelle said only what was absolutely necessary.

Pausing in front of the dress shop, Miss Sanderson peered in and spotted Irene waiting on Nettie Seton, who was running to avoirdupois and had oily skin. Glancing up, Irene waved and Miss Sanderson waved back.

So much for my detecting, she thought as she climbed the slope toward the church. Perhaps she could spot a neighbor and try a bit more. But not a soul was stirring around the vicarage or the cluster of cottages. She'd

reached the gate of the Markham house when she heard
her name called. She swung around and saw the same man
she had seen the previous day trundling his wheelchair up
the walk. He wore a tweed cap, a heavy jacket, and a
matching tartan muffler and rug. Over one arm of his chair
a heavy leather satchel hung. She walked back to him.
"Tried to catch up with you earlier but couldn't," he
panted. "I can beat anyone on a downslope but not on a
rise." He stuck out a hand only fractionally smaller than
the baker's. "I'm your neighbor, Matthew Johnston."

Miss Sanderson told him truthfully she was delighted to
meet him. He swung his gate open. "Care to come in for
tea, Miss Sanders?"

Again she told him she would be delighted and followed
him along the short walk to the ramp. She put a hand on
the back of the chair but he shook his head. "Must let me
do it myself."

He wheeled the chair up the ramp and unlocked the
yellow door. They went into a small sitting room that
managed to look larger because it was so bare. There were
only a television set, an end table, and one armchair. The
room had lovely proportions and a charming fireplace. She
pictured it with chintz, a touch of brass, mellow wood.
Her host must have guessed her thoughts. "Shame, isn't it?
Could be a nice home. But I have few visitors and don't
need much for myself. Come into the kitchen. That's
where I spend most of my time."

The kitchen was rather nice. Old oak cupboards lined
one wall and in a nook was a table covered with a bright
plastic throw and one straight-backed chair. On the win-
dowsill was a red geranium. From one side of the room a
bedroom opened, from the other a bath. The room
smelled deliciously of spices and baking. "You're lucky,"

Johnston told her. "Baked this morning and have fresh currant buns. Sometimes I pick up something from the bakery but mainly I do it myself. Helps pass the time." Taking off his cap and jacket, he hung them on low pegs. As he draped the muffler over the jacket he patted it affectionately. "Gillian and Paul gave me this rug last Christmas and had the boys give me the muffler. Laid them away because they're pure wool and figured they were too good to use everyday. But after they . . . after they were gone I got them out and threw away my old rug and scarf. Wish now I'd worn them sooner so they could . . ."

"I understand," Miss Sanderson told him gently. "You were close to my cousin's family."

"They made me feel like a member of their family. Hang your duds over there, Miss Sanders. Had a couple of higher hooks left for visitors. You take that chair and I'll get tea on. No, I don't need any help and from what I've heard you can use a rest after shopping. Shouldn't be lugging groceries like that."

"I'm having most of the shopping delivered, Mr. Johnston—"

"Mind calling me Matthew? Gillian always called me that and the boys called me Uncle Matt."

"If you'll call me Abigail."

She watched while he boiled water and measured tea leaves. The fixtures were all normal height but he used only the lower cupboards and the lowest shelf on the fridge. She guessed he used only the front burners on the stove. "Wouldn't it be handier to have those lowered?" she asked.

"Rented house. Can't change much. Owner did let me install metal bars in the bedroom and bath to swing myself around on. I make out fine. Don't need much space for supplies anyway." He put the teapot, cups, and plates on a tray, deposited it on his lap, and wheeled his chair to the table. Miss Sanderson made no effort to assist. Returning to the counter for a plate of buns and a butter dish, he rolled his chair opposite hers.

"Seems nice to have company, Abigail. It's been lonely lately. Went over to the Markham house a couple of times after Irene moved in to see whether I could help out but Mrs. Toogood didn't need me. When Gillian was alive it was different. Helped out all the time then. Mended furniture and things—once I was a carpenter—and tried to take the boys off her hands. Used to take them down to the shops with me. Arthur and Andrew always coaxed to go to the chemist's for an ice cream." He poured the tea. "All past now. No sense in dwelling on it."

"Have you lived here long?"

"Newcomer to Maddersley and the locals don't let me forget it. Have to have had your family here for generations to be one of them. But Jericho Lane's chock-full of outsiders. I arrived over a year ago, about the time Irene Markham came back and started her shop. The vicar's been here about ten years and Miss Beauchamp—she's the cottage with the red door—came about six months ago." He chuckled. "Even Nurse Ines is considered an outsider and she came with Paul when he set up practice here."

"The young chap at the inn—Paddy Rourke—has he been here long?"

"Born here. When his dad came to Maddersley he tore the old inn down and put up a new building. That would be about thirty years ago. Paddy senior passed away but his wife Kate and his son run the place. Villagers have accepted them. I suppose because they have the only inn and Paddy's a nice young fellow."

"When I arrived yesterday he was kind to me."

"Heard he sent Rog Austin up with your bag." Johnston laughed. "Can see from your expression you never lived in a place this size. Drop a pin in the Fox and Crow and we hear it in Jericho Lane."

Munching a tasty bun, Miss Sanderson ran over the information she had about this man. His home had been in Gloucester, Cheltenham to be exact. Ten years ago he'd lost his only child and not a year later had been crippled in an automobile accident. His wife had died in the same accident. Only good things were said about him in the police report. Honest, hardworking, decent, his word as good as a legal contract. She regarded him sadly. A fine reward for a good life—crippled and quite alone. At one time he must have been a big man. He had powerful sloping shoulders, a massive chest, and thick arms. But his legs, outlined in red and green and yellow plaid looked like twisted sticks. His hair was snow-white and cropped short. Traces of a ginger color still lingered in his brows and lashes. His brow was noble and his blue eyes still youthful but his face was deeply furrowed and he looked much older than his recorded age. The furrows, she decided, came more from suffering than age.

He regarded her with sympathy. "It must be hard for you to mourn people you never met."

"It is. I feel like a stranger here. I know so little about them and I suppose I feel . . . guilty."

"There's always that feeling of guilt when it's too late. I still feel guilty about my daughter's death. Ariel died young, only nineteen. Just starting her life."

"Was she killed in an accident?"

"You mean this?" He touched a knee. "No, this happened afterward. When Ariel got sick she was living in

London. Came home to us and I was all for calling the doctor but her mother put her to bed and Ariel seemed some better. Just had a pain on one side. Turned out to be a ruptured appendix and my girl died before we could get her to the hospital. Dr. Brown felt as bad as Julia and I. He'd delivered her and Ariel was his goddaughter. Here, I'll show you her picture." He pulled a framed picture from a drawer. "Ariel and her mother taken about a year before we lost her."

There were two women in the picture, both slender, dark, with misty hair, looking like twins and with a fragile haunting type of beauty. "My family," Johnston said proudly. "Folks were always surprised a rough fellow like me would have a family like that. Julia came from a wealthy background and had a good education. Musical. She played the piano like you wouldn't believe. She passed talent on to Ariel . . . girl was studying ballet at a school in London when it happened. Teachers told us Ariel would have been a marvelous dancer if she'd lived."

Johnston ran a thick finger over the pictured faces. "Couldn't believe a lovely creature like Julia would want me. Family tried to break us up and when we married they cut Julia right off. I felt bad but Julia always told me, 'Matthew, I'd give up the world to be your wife.'" He sighed. "That's what she did. Gave her world up for me. I earned a good living and took good care of both of them. If it'd helped them I would have ripped my skin off. Then . . . I lost them both."

"Did your wife die in the accident that—"

"Yes. She was driving our car. That guilt you mentioned. My fault she was at the wheel. Should have known better. Julia never got over Ariel's death. Dr. Brown warned me she was . . . disturbed, he called it. But I hated driving and Julia loved to. So, I let her get behind the wheel and she wrecked the car deliberately."

Miss Sanderson gasped and he nodded his white head. "On purpose, Abigail. She didn't want to live. Wanted both of us to die. Well, she got part of her wish. Me . . . often I wish Julia had gotten it all."

Sadness overwhelmed Miss Sanderson. What right, she thought, have I to come into this bare house and pry into this man's life? But Johnston was speaking rapidly, as though welcoming a chance to talk. "I stayed on in our home, coping as best I could. We had friends and they tried to help but even friends drift away in time from a cripple. Finally last year Dr. Brown—funny I've known him all my life and never called him by his first name— anyway, he told me I had to get away from that house, out of that city. Told me it was slowly killing me. Asked where I could go and Dr. Brown tells me anywhere, just go. So I did. Rented this house and moved in next to the Fosters. For this past year I thought the doctor was right. I found myself another family, a second chance at life."

"Matthew, I'm glad my relatives were kind to you."

"*Kind*. They were wonderful. Paul took care of me all the time and wouldn't take a penny in payment. Gillian welcomed me in their house anytime I wanted to go. Had me over to dinner every week. Baked things and ran over with them. Gave me that geranium. They even had a ramp built up to their back porch so I could come and go. And the children—" Breaking off, he covered his face with big carpenter's hands. "Then I lost *them*. In one night they were gone. You've no idea what it's been like."

"No, I don't. I've never lost one family, let alone two." She made a move to rise. "I'm sorry I upset you, Matthew. I'd better go."

"No, please don't. Does me good to talk. Nobody to talk to now." His hands fell away from his face and youthful eyes drilled into hers. "You're going to be told a lot of wild tales in the village. Folks are going to be filling your ears with filthy things about Paul and Gillian. May have started already."

"They have. I heard something about Melanie—"

"Lies, all lies! The Fosters hardly laid to rest and those vultures tearing at them!" With an effort he composed himself. "Paul worshipped his wife. He never put a hand on that girl. Gillian and he were sorry for the child. Ernie Marlow is a brute. Goes to the Fox and Crow and then beats his family. The Fosters took the girl as a live-in maid to help Mrs. Toogood out. Ernie didn't like it but figured it would keep his daughter in the village, where he could get at her. But he beat her once too often and Paul, he took a look at the bruises and tells Gillian we've got to get Melanie away before Ernie kills her. So the Fosters gave the girl some money and sneaked her off to London. Melanie wanted to be a hairdresser, you see."

Johnston scowled. "They did a good turn and what did they get for it? Ernie Marlow and Nell Austin and that good-for-nothing son of hers were after them something fierce. Came right into the house when Paul was out and lit into Gillian. When it happened I was in the kitchen and I was going right into the living room and straighten them out. But I didn't have to. Gillian stood right up to them and told them they couldn't force her to tell them where Melanie was. Ernie threatened to call in the police and Gillian said 'Go ahead; the police will be after you when Paul tells them how badly Melanie was beaten.' Then Ernie and Nell and Rog all started yelling and Gillian ordered them out or she would ring up the police herself." With satisfaction, Johnston added, "They got out fast. Knew she was spunky enough to do it."

This version of the Austin-Marlow-Foster feud sounded much different from the one that Mary Maddersley had told her. Miss Sanderson sent out a feeler. "Another name was mentioned, Matthew. Beauchamp, I believe."

He waved a dismissing hand. "Linda Beauchamp was Paul's patient. High-strung girl with nervous problems. Nothing but back-fence chitchat."

She came in from another angle. "When did this quarrel over Melanie Marlow take place?"

"Let's see." He rubbed his square chin. "Must've been just before the dog poisonings. That's right. Gillian threw them out on Friday and the dogs were poisoned the following Monday. Ugly business. Have a suspicion maybe Ernie Marlow had a hand in that. Hitting back at the Fosters."

Dog poisoning was news to Miss Sanderson. No mention had been made of that in the police reports. "The Fosters had a dog poisoned?"

"An Alsatian, big brute called Wolf. Looked like a wolf and acted like one too. He was Gillian's dog. Didn't like Paul or the children. Growled when the boys tried to pat him. I suppose he would have had to have been put down anyway but Gillian was all broken up. She loved that dog and Wolf was crazy about her."

"Were other dogs poisoned?"

"Two more. One of Paddy Rourke's old terriers and Dora Campbell's Peke. Paddy really got his Irish up about his dog. Said if he could prove who did it he would go after the poisoner with a gun."

"How long was this before the Fosters died?"

"About a month. Why? You think there might be a con-
nection?"

"If the Alsatian had been alive that night it would have
been difficult for anyone to have harmed the family."

"To harm Gillian, anyway. You know, Abigail, you
could be onto something. Maybe I should ring up that
Sergeant Brummell and tell him."

"Someone else may have mentioned it to the police,"
Miss Sanderson suggested, knowing full well no one had.

"I don't think anyone did. But it wasn't just Gillian's dog
that was killed. Why kill the other two?"

"What better way to conceal the real target?"

"Hey!" He gave her a wide admiring smile. "Abigail,
maybe you missed your calling. Should have been a detective. By the way, what work do you do?"

"Not much." She gave him details on the real cousin's
life. "I've never had any financial reason to work. Oh, I'm
on various committees and help out with charity drives and
that sort of thing. But I do . . . or did a great deal of
traveling when my health was better."

"Irene didn't mention what you suffer from."

A superstitious dread kept her from saying the name of
the disease that was slowly wasting Abigail Sanders away.
She improvised. "A number of ailments. A wonky
heart . . ." She touched her chest. "Blood pressure, a thyroid condition. As long as I get proper rest and diet I manage to get by fairly well."

"See you look after yourself. Shouldn't think coming
down here at this time would be good for you."

Leaning back in her chair, she touched the red bloom
on the geranium. "I had to. Irene and little Lucy are my
only living relatives."

"I understand." He reached out a hand and patted hers.

She noticed again the size of that hand. It must be almost twice the size of her own.

"Would you . . . would it disturb you to tell me about the last day?"

"Do you really want to know?"

"I feel I must."

He hefted the teapot. "I'll make fresh." As he wheeled around the kitchen he told her his memories about the Fosters' last day. "It was the day before Arthur's birthday but I guess you know that. Gillian was as excited about the party as the boys were. She was in the family way again and hadn't been feeling chipper, so I went over shortly after lunch to see whether I could help. She was tickled to death I came. Showed me a list of things she had to do. She sent the boys up to their room to play so we could get things ready. Paul was in the surgery looking after the patients and Mrs. Toogood was bustling around.

"Nurse Ines was there too?"

"She never missed a day. Even if she was sick she thought Paul couldn't get on without her. That day she *was* sick. Nurse Ines had a dilly of a cold and had given it to Lucy. I remember telling Gillian it might be better if the nurse did stay off when she was ailing and Gillian laughed and said the blasted woman would drag herself to the office if her leg was broken." His eyes looked past Miss Sanderson, at something she couldn't see. "We worked at the table in the kitchen, Gillian and I. Soon's we had something finished we would put it in the laundry room where the boys couldn't spot it. I blew up about three dozen balloons with a little pump while Gillian made up paper and ribbon baskets for the candy. Then she cut out the letters for the Happy Birthday streamer and had me put paste and glitter stuff on them. We made the party

hats too. Pirate hats for the boys and tiny crown things for
the girls. Gillian called them . . ."

"Tiaras."

"That's the word." He smiled, lost in a memory he was
enjoying. "Gillian told me she was making one up for little
Lucy and I said the baby would either try to eat it or rip it
up. She smiled and said when she was a little girl her
daddy always called her a princess and on her birthdays
she always had a tiara. It was a good afternoon."

"Cozy," Miss Sanderson said, hiding a shiver.

"About four, Gillian said I was looking tired and I'd better get home and rest. I offered to stay on and help but she
said she didn't have much to do, just some baking, and she
could do that after the boys were in bed."

"The cake, I suppose."

"No, Irene was bringing that up. Had it made up special
at the bakery. Arthur was mad about planes and Ernie
Marlow was putting a toy plane on it with clouds and sky
and everything. But Gillian was going to make up some
gingerbread men and some pigs in a blanket. Arthur loved
both. I was wheeling out of the kitchen to get my coat
when Mrs. Toogood brought the baby down and put her
in the playpen. Mrs. Toogood said she figured the baby
should be bedded down soon, and Gillian picked Lucy up
and hugged her. She said no. Lucy seemed better and she
would keep her up until the boys went to bed. Laughed
and said that way maybe the baby would sleep straight
through and let her get some rest. Mrs. Toogood said she
hoped so because the next day was going to be tiring with
eight kiddies racing around. I wheeled down the hall to
the closet and the telephone rang so I answered it. It was
Irene. I called Gillian and she started to talk so I got my

coat on and waved goodbye to her. She waved back . . . and she blew me a kiss. That was the last I saw of her."

He bowed his head and Miss Sanderson looked sadly at him. After a moment he raised his head and the blue eyes were blurred with tears. "I came back here and wrapped up my present for Arthur. I'd gotten him a kit for a model airplane, a Spitfire. Too old for the lad but I was going to help him put it together. Then I went in there—" He pointed toward the sitting room. "—and sat by the window. Thinking about the next day. I was looking forward to the party. Gillian had asked me over to help with the children, and I guess I was feeling a little sad too."

"Why?"

"Because it would be the last birthday party I would go to in that house."

"You had a premonition?"

"Didn't Irene tell you the Fosters were leaving Maddersley?"

Irene hadn't but Miss Sanderson knew all about it. She shook her head. "Didn't say a word about it. Where were they going?"

"To London. Paul had always wanted to set up practice there. Gillian wasn't quite as eager but he persuaded her it would be much better for the children than to be raised in a village. They'd bought a nice home in a good district and were nearly ready to go. They were going to either rent the Markham house or have Irene move in and look after it."

"It takes quite a sum of money to set up a fashionable practice in London. Was it Gillian's—"

"No. She spent most of her inheritance fixing the house

up. A few months ago Paul came into a large inheritance—"

"Irene said his family were poor."

"His godfather wasn't and when he died everything went to Paul."

"Then Lucy is an heiress."

He nodded his head and said with a touch of malice, "Which may be why Paul's brother Leonard is so anxious to get back and look after the baby. Be sizable allotments for the guardian of that little girl."

"Does the Markham house go to Lucy too?"

"That's Irene's now. Their father was a fair man and left the house entailed. On Gillian's death it was to be her sister's."

"How did you feel about the Fosters leaving?"

"Terrible at first. Kind of deserted. I'd gotten so used to going over and I was so fond of the boys and everything. But Paul and Gillian cheered me up. Told me I would be welcome to visit in London anytime. Wouldn't have been the same, though."

"No. You would have missed them." Miss Sanderson glanced at her watch. "How time has flown. I must get back and start dinner." She put a hand on his sloping shoulder. "Matthew, you've been wonderful. I feel now as though I had known my cousin and her family. You've brought them to life. They sound like such an ideal family. I can't see why anyone would want them dead."

"Neither can I." He gazed up at her. "But this is a bad world now, Abigail. Maybe there's someone who couldn't bear to see them so happy. I don't know. I don't know much about anything anymore. But I'm going to tell you three things and you better listen."

She stared down at him and he said heavily, "Look after yourself. Let Irene and Mrs. Toogood do the work over there. You're doing your bit by being there to keep Irene company. You've asked a lot of questions. I know you want the person who did that caught as much as I do but let the police handle it. And, Abigail, keep those doors locked."

In a brown study, Miss Sanderson walked the few yards to the Markham house. The same warning. Lock the doors. They come from outside, Irene had said, with knives.

SEVEN

IRENE KICKED OFF HER shoes and curled up like a cat in a brown velour chair. Shaking short hair back from her face, she smiled at Miss Sanderson. "Your cook's lessons must have taken, Abigail. Dinner was tasty. I'd almost forgotten what decent food was like." Miss Sanderson gestured toward the scotch bottle and Irene shuddered. "Not for me, I'm a reformed sinner. I was so hungover this morning I could barely stagger to work. Felt rather foolish too. Nothing like you coming here and finding no food and a drunken hostess."

"Probably did you good. You were wound up like a spring."

"It probably did." Irene asked casually, "Did I babble a lot of nonsense last night? I can't remember much about the latter part of the evening."

"I thought you made sense."

"What did I talk about?"

"This and that. Your youth. Gillian. About the men who were disappointed when she married so suddenly."

"They've probably recovered. That was years ago."

"You didn't mention names."

The answer was a shrug. Miss Sanderson decided to do a little probing but Irene had a question to ask her. "Mrs. Toogood tells me you're giving her lunch tomorrow. Is that true?"

"I plan to. Any objections?"

"Nary a one unless she gets the idea she's going to make a habit of eating here. But I can't see how you can possibly have taken a fancy to that woman."

"She hasn't taken my fancy but Lucy has and you must admit Mrs. Toogood takes good care of the baby."

"That's what she's paid for. By the way, Dora Campbell dropped in to pick up a sweater—"

"Lavender, I'll bet."

"Close. Lilac. Dora said you'd had lunch at her tearoom and had met our lady of the manor. How did you like Mary Maddersley?"

"She's a forthright person. Invited me for tea tomorrow."

"My, what an honor."

"On my way home I met Matthew Johnston."

"Who told you what a paragon Gillian was. Abigail, I don't want you encouraging that man to start coming over here again. When I moved in I gave Mrs. Toogood to understand he wasn't welcome."

"Don't you like him?"

"It's not a matter of like or dislike. I don't want him making a nuisance of himself like he did with Paul and my sister."

"They considered Matthew a nuisance?"

"If they didn't they should have. He was in and out all the time. Acted like it was his house. It happens to be mine now and I won't stand for it."

"He seems a harmless old man. Terribly lonely."

"Most people are."

Miss Sanderson studied the younger woman. A sober Irene was going to be much harder to handle than Irene in her cups. She was cool and controlled and rather wary. The milky eyes looked like small hard marbles. Those eyes snapped to Miss Sanderson. "What on earth are you doing?" Irene asked.

Realizing she was clicking her thumbnail against a front tooth, Miss Sanderson guiltily dropped her hand into her lap. She thought of Robby who had complained for years about that mannerism. "A bad habit. I do it quite unconsciously when I'm thinking."

"You seem to do a lot of thinking, Abigail, and you ask too many questions. Even Dora Campbell commented on that—how curious you are."

"*Curious.*" Time for some well-feigned anger. Jumping to her feet, Miss Sanderson started to stride up and down the salmon carpet. "This attitude of yours and the villagers makes me believe you don't want to think or ask questions. Oh, it's sad but let's forget about it. Sweep it under the carpet. Irene, four people died in this house and no one seems to give a damn!" She paused to catch her breath and found she wasn't acting; she *was* angry. "Those people happen to have been my relatives and I *care.*"

"We all care but the police are handling it."

"How much help are they getting? Did *you* try to help them?"

The marble eyes dropped and a flush crept up the woman's thin cheeks. "I couldn't bring myself to repeat gossip about Gillian. We didn't get along too well but she was my *sister.*"

"Look!" Pulling to a halt, Miss Sanderson glared down at the other woman. "The murderer didn't drop in out of the blue. Gillian and Paul and their sons were killed by some-

one in this village. The answer to their murders lies in the
past, in who hated them enough to kill horribly. That is
not gossip."

Irene threw up an arm as though warding off a blow.
"Please, Abigail, no more. It's so frightening. Every person
I see, every person I talk to . . . I think, Is it you; Are you
the one? I'm terrified. I've no one I can trust."

I've got her on the run, Miss Sanderson thought, and
dropped back on her chair. She patted Irene's hand. "My
dear, you know you can trust me."

"I think I'll have that drink now." She made a move to
get up but Miss Sanderson waved her back. She made up a
drink, heavy on scotch, light on soda. As she handed the
glass over, Irene asked meekly, "What do you want to
know?"

"Names. The men in Gillian's past who you said were
'led down the garden path.'"

"Dr. Clay and—"

"The vicar?"

"Yes. And Sir Donald Maddersley and Paddy Rourke.
Gillian worked part-time for all of them and they were
mad about her—"

"What kind of work?"

"Typing for Sir Donald and the vicar, books for Paddy.
To put in her time, I suppose. Gillian wasn't much good at
that type of work but she was so pretty I don't suppose
they cared how efficient she was."

"And each of them thought she loved *him?*"

"Gillian had a way about her. She could make anyone
think she adored him. Didn't I tell you that last night?"

"Three men," Miss Sanderson mused. "At the same time
in a place this size. Gillian must have been a charmer."

"If she'd wanted to I swear she could have charmed birds from trees."

"When did these men find out about her marriage plans?"

"Not until after she and Paul were married."

"Blimey. How did they react?"

"Paddy got drunk and stayed that way for a week. He also hurt his hand. Alfred Austin told me he smashed it through a window in the inn."

"Were you in the village at that time?"

"No, but the villagers have long memories. When I set up shop last year they were willing to tell all. According to Dora Campbell Sir Donald went right off his head and—"

"Yesterday she hinted he was . . . She said, 'not right in the head.'"

"Dora has a vicious tongue."

"He isn't mad?"

"Of course not. Sir Donald has nervous problems and must live quietly but he certainly isn't mad. Why, he's written a number of books on gardening and even does a column about it for the newspaper. Does that sound mad?"

Depends on the type of madness, Miss Sanderson thought. "How did the vicar react?"

"For a man of the cloth rather violently." Irene's lips twitched in a smile. "Preached a couple of sermons that were dandies. Rather glad I wasn't in the congregation. Mrs. Toogood said Dr. Clay ranted on about prostitutes—" Her brow crinkled in thought. "No, she said strumpets. She said he kept using a quotation about strumpets and plague. Anyway, although Dr. Clay didn't mention Gillian by name, all the villagers knew who he was raving about."

"Plague. Strumpet," Miss Sanderson muttered. Then she

had it. "'Tis the strumpet's plague,'" she quoted slowly, "'To beguile many and be beguiled by one.'"

Blue marble eyes widened and Irene asked. "The Bible?"

"The Bard. *Othello*, to be exact. I've a friend who quotes Shakespeare continuously." Robby, Miss Sanderson thought longingly, how I wish you were here quoting Shakespeare right now. "I suppose we can cross those three men off the suspect list. The murderer had to have had access to Paul's office to get the drug—"

"How do you know that?"

How did she know it? Miss Sanderson wondered wildly. She grasped at the obvious. "It was reported in the news accounts that the drug came from a cupboard in the surgery."

"So it was. I'd forgotten. But Paddy and Sir Donald and the vicar were Paul's patients and they could easily have taken the drug."

"The way they felt about Gillian and her marriage to Paul . . . and they were *his* patients?"

"The nearest doctor is in Lambert and he's old and quite doddering and never was much good anyway. As I said, this all happened over six years ago. None of those men would hold a grudge that long."

What about you? Miss Sanderson asked silently. You've held a grudge against your sister since you were a child. Aloud she said, "I want to hear about this house. Why does it have a bad reputation?"

Evidently Irene had decided to cooperate. She answered readily. "Because the villagers are a bunch of ninnies. You can't blame a building for what happens in it. There've been a number of unrelated tragedies here and the superstitious idiots blame this house for it. That's why father was able to buy it so cheaply. Our family house is on the way to Maddersley Hall but it's huge and needed so many repairs. My parents couldn't afford to keep it on so we moved in here when Gillian was three and I was ten."

"These tragedies . . ."

"The man who built it received a head wound in the Second World War and he killed his wife. Apparently he was terribly jealous of her and suffered from the delusion she was being unfaithful to him. They found her body in the drawing room—that's the surgery now—and the man confessed. He was put in a mental home." She rubbed her chin. "I can't recall his name. Then a middle-aged couple from Leeds bought the house and one night their maid was killed—at the foot of the staircase. The police thought she'd interrupted a burglary but they never found the killer. The couple, I think their name was Hawes, rented the house to a young woman from London. I remember her vaguely. Quite pretty. She was an artist and ran with a tacky crowd. Another artist, a man, came to visit and they must have quarreled. He killed her. After that the Hawes were glad to sell to my parents."

Miss Sanderson became aware that her thumb was noisily drumming against her teeth again. Folding her hands in her lap, she asked, "How were they killed?"

"Stabbed."

"All of them?"

The brown head bobbed and Miss Sanderson gulped. From outside . . . with knives. She was tempted to jump up and check the doors. "You do plan to stay on here."

"Of course. It's my home."

"Won't it be lonely after Lucy's guardian comes for her—"

"How do you know that?" Irene snapped. "That fact certainly wasn't reported in newspapers."

"Matthew told me."

"That busybody! Hears all, sees all, tells all. I suppose he also told you Lucy is inheriting a good-sized estate."

"He did."

It was Irene's turn to jump up and pace up and down. "The whole thing is so unfair. I should have been my niece's guardian. When the solicitor read the will and he said Leonard and Marjorie Foster were to have Lucy I simply couldn't believe it. They have so much now. Leonard has a good job and they travel to so many interesting places. And they have. *three* children." She swung on Miss Sanderson. "Do you think it's fair?"

"It's a responsibility raising a child. How could you keep your shop on?"

"I wouldn't have to. Lucy's guardian receives a generous allowance. And I can't possibly keep a house like this on the tiny income I make from the shop."

"Perhaps Leonard Foster would be happy to let you care for the child. Why don't you ask him?"

"I have. He rang up after he heard about his brother and Gillian and I suggested just that. He said no, Marjorie and he are better qualified to raise Lucy. He said they're making arrangements to take her off my hands." Irene scowled. "*Qualified.* Their children are spoiled rotten."

"Did you expect to be the children's guardian?"

"I didn't *expect* anything. I didn't expect young healthy people like Gillian and Paul to die before I did. But I have a right to my niece. Wasn't Paul's will unfair?"

"Totally," Miss Sanderson agreed tactfully. "If anything were to happen to Lucy, what about Paul's estate?"

Slumping back in the armchair, Irene said, "Split between the next of kin."

"Leonard Foster and you?"

"Yes." She asked tartly, "Do you suspect *me*?"

"Of course not. I was only—" Miss Sanderson broke off.
She'd been about to say curious. "I was only wondering. So
. . . if Lucy had died that night you and Leonard would
have inherited."

"But she didn't. When I found her alive I couldn't believe
it. I thought she must be dead too."

"Tell me about that night."

"Must I?"

"Yes."

All fight seemed to have gone out of the other woman.
"I've told this over and over again. You'd think repetition
would blunt the horror. It doesn't." She took a deep
breath. "Very well, Abigail, into the breach once more. I
rang up a few minutes after four in the afternoon. I'd
planned to come directly here after I closed the shop to
give my sister a hand with the party preparations. Gillian
wasn't having an easy pregnancy this time and she tired so
easily. But at the last minute I found I had to do alterations
on a suit for Mary Maddersley and I would have to work
late.

"Matthew answered the telephone and Gillian came on.
I told her I would be delayed until after nine and she said
not to worry. Matthew had helped her out that afternoon
and all she had left to do was a bit of baking. She asked
whether I'd picked up the cake from the bakery and was it
nice. I said yes, it was lovely and Ernie had put a toy
plane—"

"Matthew told me about the cake decorations."

Irene held out her glass and while Miss Sanderson attended to it she continued, "Then we chatted for a bit—"

"What about?"

"The party. Gillian said she and Paul were giving Arthur a small radio for his bedroom and that Matthew had bought him a model plane kit. I laughed and told her I'd bought Arthur a plane kit too and she said Matthew would help the boy put both of them together. She sounded tired so I advised her not to bother too much with dinner— Gillian and Paul always dined in the dining room and she fussed over meals. She told me she intended to make a simple meal that night, steak and salad, and they'd eat at the kitchen table. I warned her not to get overtired and she laughed and said not to be a mother hen. Said both Matthew and Paul were fussing over her enough. Then we rang off."

Irene paused and applied herself to her drink. Watching her, Miss Sanderson hoped it wouldn't have as rapid and disastrous an effect as the drinks had had the previous evening. "Do you know what time you got here?"

"I should. I went over and over that with the police. I finished the alterations up a few minutes before nine. As I left the shop I looked at my watch and it was nine sharp. It didn't take me long to get here. It had been raining earlier and was raw and cold and I was hurrying. Pockets of ice were forming on the walks. I was tired and chilled and was lugging my gift and the cake. All I wanted to do was deliver them and get back to bed. I didn't notice lights at Miss Beauchamp's cottage or Nurse Ines' but I could see a light on in Matthew's sitting room. I went up to the door here and—"

"Which door?"

"The kitchen door. I expected to find Gillian in the kitchen. I took the walk that runs between Matthew's cottage and this side of the house. I knocked—"

"Surely your sister would have left it unlocked for you."

"Not in this house," Irene said grimly. "Mother and father drilled it into both of us about locking doors. Anyway, I could see a line of light between the curtains but there was no answer. I did try the door and it was locked—"

"You didn't have a key?"

"The only people who had keys were Gillian and Paul. Another of my parents' rules. And if you're wondering whether I had a key left from when I lived here, the answer is no. After his marriage Paul had new locks put on."

"And after you tried the door?"

"I knew Gillian wasn't in the kitchen. Lucy had been sick with a cold so I thought Gillian was upstairs with the baby. I put the packages down on the porch and trotted down the ramp and back the way I had come. Again I noticed the light in Matthew's cottage. I ran up on the veranda and rang the chimes. There was the light in the living room and I could hear music. I thought Paul must be relaxing and watching a television program. Again no one answered."

"Were you worried by this time?"

Irene considered. Then she shook her head and hair spilled away from her face. "Annoyed. After all, I was expected. I wondered whether Paul and Gillian could have dropped over to see Matthew and then I thought, no, they would never leave the children alone. So I decided to try the side door, the one to the surgery . . ."

Her voice trailed off and Miss Sanderson envisioned that dreadful evening. Irene, muffled in anorak and knitted hat, angered at being kept out in the cold, tired and wanting only her bed, making her way around the house, up the walk to the steps that led to the surgery. Irene said slowly, "I slipped on the bottom step and looked down. There was a glaze of ice on it. These are steep steps and can be treacherous. I grabbed at the door handle and it—the door—swung open. It had been left ajar.

"That was when I got worried. After the last patient left Nurse Ines always locked that door. And Gillian always checked it afterward. That annoyed Paul's nurse. She figured the surgery was *her* territory. I think . . . I remember calling Paul's name. Then I turned around to close and lock the door and I saw marks on the woodwork around it. They were red and moist and for a moment I thought they were paint. I wiped a finger through them and knew it wasn't paint . . . it was blood."

No longer did Irene's eyes look like blue marbles. They were filled with terror. Her glass was empty again so Miss Sanderson took it from her hand and went to the gateleg table. This time she splashed a considerable amount of soda on the single malt. Should she force this woman to relive the nightmare? Then she knew she must. Perhaps Irene would remember something, some tiny thing she hadn't told the police. Closing Irene's fingers around the glass, she said, "Go on."

"It's easy enough for you," Irene said brokenly. "You never knew them. Gillian was my young sister and Paul—once I'd loved him."

"It's not easy for either of us," Miss Sanderson told her sternly. "But it must be done."

Taking a long swallow, Irene said jerkily, "The door to his office was open and I could see him. There was so much blood and things protruded from his chest. They were his—"

"I can guess what they were."

"I ran into the hall and heard the music from the living room. Before I saw the boys I saw that television screen. Silly little figures dancing. Arthur and Andrew looked like they were asleep. The fire was burning. I ran to the kitchen and I found . . . Gillian. I remember standing over her, thinking that the murderer might still be in the house. I threw open the back door and tripped over the cake."

"But you didn't run from the house?"

"Lucy! I thought, she's dead too. Run! I couldn't. I went back up the hall. The shadows seemed to move and I was so frightened I could hardly move. Then I heard Lucy cry out." Irene shook her head. "I must have gone upstairs and picked her up. I can't remember doing it. The next thing I knew I was at Matthew's back door and he opened it and took the baby and called the police and a doctor came and gave me a shot and . . ."

Irene was tearing a paper hankie into bits. Miss Sanderson took the scraps and threw them onto the grate. She put a comforting arm around the younger woman's thin, shaking shoulders. "I'll help you up to bed."

Whether it was the drink or the memories Miss Sanderson had no idea but Irene Markham did need help. She found pajamas, helped Irene into them, eased her into bed, and pulled the duvet to her chin. She rested a hand on Irene's brow. "Sleep," she told the woman. "You're safe. I'm right here."

Lashes drifted down and Miss Sanderson waited until Irene's breathing deepened into a soft snoring sound. Then she walked to the door and put her hand on the switch. Before the lights snapped off she took a long look at the portraits of the Foster family. Their eyes seemed to coldly examine her. Can you find the one? she fancied they were asking. I don't know, Miss Sanderson told them silently, but I'm sure as hell trying.

She went to the nursery and stood over the crib. The rosy nightlight showed a chubby hand gripping a teddy bear in a red sweater. With a tender finger she touched a warm moist cheek.

As she closed the door of the nursery she glanced down the hall at double doors. It would have been simple, she thought, for Irene to have made two trips to the Markham house that night—the first to commit the murders, the second to have discovered the bodies. If Irene had murdered for hate and profit she was an amazing actress.

Miss Sanderson had known murderers before. Some of them had been consummate actors. Keeping this in mind, she went to her bed.

EIGHT

MRS. TOOGOOD, HER TINY eyes bright with anticipation, sat at the kitchen table watching Miss Sanderson moving around the stove. "Decent of you, Miss Sanders, and my, haven't you done it up brown! Pork pie and beer and raspberry tart. Takes me back to when the missus, rest her soul, was alive. Always gave me a hot lunch she did. Waited on me too like you're doing. Can't believe her and Miss Irene were sisters. All *that* woman would give is the back of her hand."

Miss Sanderson cut into the greasy pie and put a large slab on one plate and a thinner wedge on another. She poured beer and set the foaming glass and the large piece of pie in front of her guest. "It's a shame you have to have cold lunches now."

"Don't have any choice, do I? First thing Miss Irene told me when she moved in is bring me own food or go hungry." Mrs. Toogood fell on her lunch and proceeded to wolf it down. Sipping beer, Miss Sanderson wondered how to get her companion talking. There was no need. Not only was the housekeeper a self-starter but she could eat and talk simultaneously. Her conversation consisted of remarks about her former mistress, all highly colored and complimentary. "Give me all her boys' clothes, she did, soon's they grew out of them. Some good as new and fit my Percy and Willy fine. Every Christmas the missus give me a check. Always told me to see the kiddies have a good Christmas. Give me stuff of little Lucy too for my Mollie." She buried her mouth in beer suds and her voice became muffled. "Couldn't ask for a finer lady than the missus."

Most commendable, Miss Sanderson thought, but of no help. She threw out some bait. "From what I've heard not everyone in the village agrees with you."

"Ah, that'll be the Austins and the Marlows, miss." She looked longingly at the pie dish and Miss Sanderson lifted the last slice onto her plate. "Thanks. Goes down good with beer." Taking the hint, her companion refilled the glass. "That was a sad day for the missus when she took that Marlow brat under her roof. Told the missus, no good will come of this, but missus wouldn't listen. Always felt sorry for Ernie saddled with that Maybelle as a wife and then getting a daughter like Melanie."

"I heard he abused both of them. Yesterday when I stopped in the bakery I noticed Mrs. Marlow had a bruise under her eye. And he's such a hulking brute."

"His looks is against him, miss. If Ernie looked harmless like Alfred Austin no one would think the worst of him for cuffing his women around. Poor man's only trying to keep them decent. Maybelle's always had a wandering eye, making up to anything in pants. And Melanie was worse than her mum, been after men since she was knee-high."

"But he does strike them?"

"'Course he does. Gives them a lick now and then. If'n they were mine I'd use a skillet on them. Told the missus that and she spoke real sharp to me. Tried to tell her

Melanie was lying about her dad but that girl pulled the wool over both the missus and Dr. Foster's eyes."

Mrs. Toogood had finished her second slice of pie and was eyeing her companion's untouched plate. Miss Sanderson shoved it over. "Oh no, miss, can't eat your lunch."

"I don't care that much for pork pie." Miss Sanderson added casually, "So, you sided with the Austins and Ernie Marlow?"

"Didn't side with no one. Know my place I do. But I speak my mind and the missus and Dr. Foster was dead wrong to take that girl in and then give her money to run away. Melanie's not even seventeen and heavens know what mischief she'll be up to on her own."

"And you told my cousin and her husband all this?"

"Came right out and told them. But Melanie she cried and showed them bruises and took them in. Set them right against Ernie and Nell Austin."

"And Rog Austin too."

"Rog isn't a bad lad, miss. Just says and does what his mum tells him. 'Course he had his heart set on marrying that girl and he was real upset when she left. Could use a chunk of tart now, miss."

Miss Sanderson's eyes widened. Mrs. Toogood certainly had a hearty appetite. Perhaps Irene couldn't afford to feed her if she ate this much habitually. While she cut tart and poured beer she said, "I'm surprised a girl like that could take Gillian in."

"Lot of people thought because the missus was so pretty she weren't too bright but the missus was smart enough. Melanie never took *her* in. Leastways not for long."

"But you said—"

"Said the missus wouldn't listen when she had the girl come live here. Soon's Melanie was in the house missus saw I was right. She wanted that girl outta here and away from her husband." Miss Sanderson turned and found the housekeeper regarding her shrewdly. The effect was somewhat spoiled by the large crumb dangling from her lower lip. "Doctors get a lot of females going gaga about them. 'Specially a young well set-up one like Dr. Foster. Melanie set her cap for the doctor, always rubbing up against him like. And missus had her hands full with that Miss Beauchamp. Didn't need Melanie after him too." Mrs. Toogood smiled widely and the crumb trembled and fell into her lap. "Missus handled both of them good."

Miss Sanderson took a sip of her beer. It had gone flat. "Surely my cousin could have discharged the girl."

"Wouldn't have looked good, miss. People'd be wondering why. As it was there was enough talk when Melanie left town."

"Did the doctor reciprocate Melanie's affection?"

"Huh?" The housekeeper blinked. "Oh, I see what you're getting at. Wouldn't know. I was only here days. But Melanie's a good-looking girl and it was a fine idea to get rid of her. I just didn't like the way it was done."

This version of the feud sounded more like Miss Maddersley's than Matthew Johnston's. The thought of Johnston spurred Miss Sanderson's next question. "Mr. Johnston told me he was here the day the Austins and Ernie Marlow were trying to find where Melanie had gone. Were you here too?"

"Sure was. Putting dishes in that machine right over there. Mr. Johnston was at this table, busy mending one of Andrew's toy trucks. Missus took them into the living room and didn't bother shutting the doors. They was hollering loud enough we'd heard them even if those doors had been shut. Had my hands full with Mr. Johnston. Set a lot of store by the missus he did and wanted to go in there and set them right. My, they was steamed up. Nell was yelling about the missus taking away her son's bride and Ernie was shouting about standing between a child and her parents and Rog kept yelping he'd bought the girl a ring and all." Mrs. Toogood's eyes glinted with unholy glee. "Had to grab onto Mr. Johnston's chair and hold it back. Kept telling him the missus could look after herself. She sure could too. Got rid of them and I told Mr. Johnston, 'See, missus don't need any help.' The old fellow really gave me a turn. Kinda collapsed in his chair, his shoulders all bowed, and he kept saying, 'That woman, that terrible, terrible woman!' I told him not to take on so, that Nell Austin isn't all that bad. She's got a temper and a bad mouth but she cools down fast."

Not only had Mrs. Toogood finished her lunch but also managed to finish every scrap of tart. Sitting back, she patted her stomach and stifled a belch. "When the missus come into the kitchen she sure looked pretty. Lot of color in her face and she was laughing. She says, 'I certainly told them, didn't I?' And Mr. Johnston he perked up some and didn't look so awful and he pats her hand and says, 'Gillian, you're an amazing lady.'" She shook her frowsy head. "He thought the world of the missus. Broke his heart when her and the doctor and the kiddies—" With a red-knuckled hand, the housekeeper yanked up a corner of her apron and dabbed at damp eyes. "Still can't believe it, miss. How could anyone . . ."

Miss Sanderson patted a beefy shoulder. "Have you any idea who might have done it?"

"Thought on it a lot. Don't know. Sure, there were some who didn't like them. Lot of people thought the missus was stuck-up and the boys was spoiled but you don't come in and butcher four people just 'cause you don't like them."

"Can you think of anyone who had a strong grudge against either my cousin or her husband?"

"Well, like I told you there was the Austins and Ernie—"

"Besides them."

"Some men who didn't take to the idea of the missus marrying the doctor. But they was married for years. Seems to me any of those men would have hurt them before if they was gonna. Oh, there's Dora Campbell. She still goes on about the missus taking her man away from her."

"Dora Campbell?"

"All the missus did was go out a couple of times with a chap who was courting Dora. He dropped Dora like a hot potato and who could blame him. Her with a face homely as a hedge fence. Missus sure didn't mean to break them up. Men just went wild about her. That was a long time ago too. But Dora raves on about it as though it happened yesterday."

There would have been no contest, Miss Sanderson mused, between beautiful Gillian and Dora with the sheep's face. So . . . Dora Campbell had reason to hate Gillian Foster. She was about to mention the mysterious Miss Beauchamp when the housekeeper looked at the kitchen clock and jumped to her feet. "Look at the time! Got to go up and tend to little Lucy. Tell you this, miss, only reason I stay on here is for the missus and little Lucy. Soon's the doctor's brother comes for the baby I'll be gone. Were I you I'd leave things to Miss Irene and get back to London. This house is hard enough on a body who's got her health."

"Kind of you to be concerned, Mrs. Toogood, but until Lucy leaves I'm staying."

"Suit yourself, miss." Plodding over, Mrs. Toogood swung open the door. A few words drifted back. "Nice lunch. I thank you."

Miss Sanderson sighed. All that time and food appeared to have been wasted. The only tidbit she'd gained from the housekeeper was the item about Dora Campbell. Perhaps she would fare better with Mary Maddersley. She had a couple of hours to put in before she had to arrive at the Hall. I think I'll visit the neighbors, she decided, and headed for the hall.

She was taking her coat out of the closet when Mrs. Toogood called down the stairwell, "Going out?"

"Yes, and I may not be back in time to start dinner."

"I'll tell Miss Irene. Mind you put your muffler and boots on."

Miss Sanderson decided perhaps the lunch effort was proving to have a fringe benefit. The housekeeper seemed to be mellowing. Once outside she found Mrs. Toogood's advice had been sensible. The sky was again overcast and a cold western wind was whistling. She strolled past Johnston's cottage and paused beside his neighbor's fence. A hand was pulling the curtain back in the sitting room window. Ah, Nurse Ines must be home. The blue-painted door sported an old-fashioned bellpull. She rang it lustily and the door opened wide. The woman framed in the doorway was as tall as Miss Sanderson and looked about twice as wide. She had shoulders like a rugby player. She regarded Miss Sanderson silently and with no evidence of pleasure.

"I'm Abigail Sanders, Gillian Foster's cousin."

"I know who you are. I've seen you going back and forth. Do a lot of gadding around for a sick person."

"On my doctor's orders. I've a heart condition."

Pushing wire-rimmed glasses up on a sharp nose, the nurse said, "Reasonable exercise is a good idea. So, you're the cousin who finally came to Miss Markham's aid. I always say better late than never. Don't stand there, get in. Cooling the house down. No central heating here."

No invitation was proffered to remove her coat but Miss Sanderson did it anyway. As she did she glanced around. The room was identical in shape to Johnston's but here were the chintz, mellow wood, and brass she had envisioned in his sitting room. On the grate a brisk fire radiated heat. "This is perfectly charming," she told the other woman. "What a lovely job you've done."

"Always try to make a place homey. I've had years to work on this one." Nurse Ines pointed an imperious finger. "Sit over there. Won't be in my way as I work." She strode over and continued packing books in a crate.

"Are you leaving Maddersley?"

"As soon as I finish packing and hire a van."

"But the police investigation—"

"If the police want to keep me they'll have to charge me. They've no grounds for that. I've no choice anyway. Gave my notice on this cottage for the end of this month."

"Then you must have planned to leave before the Fosters' deaths."

"When a body gets their notice they leave, don't they?"

"You weren't going to London with Dr. Foster?"

"Wasn't young enough or pretty enough for his fine new surgery. At least that's the excuse he gave." She plucked another book from the white-painted shelf, looked at it, and set it on the floor. "That's one he lent me. Have to take it back to the surgery."

Nurse Ines certainly was neither young nor pretty. She looked over fifty. She wore a baggy maroon skirt and a matching jacket. Large feet were shod in sensible black brogues and salt-and-pepper hair was strained back into a bun. In starched whites and a cap she would be impressive. Deciding on a meek approach, Miss Sanderson murmured, "What a shame. And the wonderful home you've made here, too."

"He didn't care." Apparently Miss Sanderson had hit the right note. In an aggrieved voice the nurse continued, "Doctor didn't quite put it that way. He said he would need a younger woman to handle the extra work. I'll tell you this, Miss Sanders, doctor didn't think I was too old when he was training at Guy's. Took all the help he could get from me and when he qualified and set up practice here he begged me to come down. I left everything I'd worked for—a good job with a promotion coming along, a nice comfortable flat, friends and colleagues—to come down to this dreary hole."

"Why did you do it?"

"My entire life has been devoted to medicine." Nurse Ines swung around to face her visitor. "My father was a surgeon and my mother a matron. Dr. Foster was a fine doctor. From the time he came to Guy's I knew I'd never seen a better. He was a *healer*. Down here he was absolutely wasted. Should have been in London years ago. When I heard of his plans for moving his practice I was overjoyed. Finally we were coming into our own. I had such plans for us. If I do say it myself, we were a good team."

"I imagine you were."

The last book slid into the crate and the big woman

bent, lifted it without effort, and set it against the wall. Picking up a brass bowl, she wrapped it in tissue and tucked it in a cardboard box. "When the doctor told me I wouldn't be going with him I couldn't believe my ears. Then I thought, ah, this is your wife's doing. I'm a frank woman, Miss Sanders, and I speak my mind. I didn't like your cousin and she made it quite clear she couldn't stand me. Jealous because her husband depended on me so much."

"I never knew Gillian but Mrs. Toogood tells me she was kind."

"On the surface. If it didn't cost her anything and it pleased her. She poisoned the doctor's mind against me. The moment I met her I knew she wasn't right for a doctor's wife. Took no interest in his work. All Mrs. Foster cared about was her house and gadgets for it and her children. And those children! They were little hellions."

"Not little Lucy," Miss Sanderson defended staunchly.

"Too young yet. In time she would have been like her brothers—spoiled and sassy and whining. That wasn't the doctor's fault. He had no say in raising them."

"Were you in close contact with Gillian and the children?"

"Stayed as far away from them as I could get. The surgery was my area and I made certain to keep those children *and* Mrs. Foster out of it." Nurse Ines neglected her packing and straightened, her hands planted firmly on her hips. A formidable woman, Miss Sanderson thought. The nurse continued, "Didn't even let the housekeeper in there. Told Mrs. Toogood no messing around. I did the cleaning there and kept everything in order. If I do say so myself it was always spotless."

A thought struck Miss Sanderson. "Did you clean up after . . ."

"Of course. As soon as they took the doctor's body away I went right in and started scrubbing. Couldn't do much with the rug in the office. That will have to be discarded. Blood is hard to get out of carpeting."

"Didn't you find it terrible?"

"Why should I? I'm a nurse. Cleaned up worse things than blood."

"But you knew this man; you'd worked with him for years. Surely you were fond of him."

Nurse Ines, for the first time since Miss Sanderson had been admitted to her house, smiled. At least her lips pulled back from large white teeth. "I respected the doctor's ability, not him. And I lost even that respect when he dismissed me. Threw me aside like a . . ."

"An old shoe?"

"Like a piece of rubbish. Devoted the best years of my life to that man and that was my reward. He didn't *care* about me. I was no more use to him and he didn't even care if I could find a decent job."

Miss Sanderson was struck with the horrible thought that there was a possibility that Nurse Ines had *enjoyed* scrubbing up Paul Foster's blood. "But you said you blamed Gillian for that, not Paul."

"I said I started out blaming her. I ended up blaming him. If he could be that ungrateful, that easily swayed by his wife, well . . . good riddance to bad rubbish."

Nurse Ines hadn't been exaggerating. She *was* frank. Watching the woman's powerful hands wrapping up a slender glass vase, Miss Sanderson asked, "Did you tell the police all this?"

"I told them only what was necessary. That was none of their business."

"Did anyone else know about your dismissal?"

"The only ones who knew were the doctor and Mrs. Foster. No reason for them to talk about it. The doctor's patients may not have loved me but I'll tell you straight, they respected me."

And so do I, Miss Sanderson told her silently. You're strong and capable and possibly ruthless. According to Beau Brummell the wounds in Gillian's back and her sons' had been done as a medical man might, or, perhaps, as a nurse would. Despite the heat from the fireplace she shivered and the nurse noticed. "Miss Sanders, I do hope you're not coming down with a chill."

"No, I'm just tired. I haven't been sleeping well. Strange bed, you know."

"You're in no shape to be here. I'm surprised your physician allowed it."

Miss Sanderson said simply, "I had to come."

Rugby shoulders shrugged and Nurse Ines reached for a handsome ormolu clock. "Well, you know what they say good intentions lead to." She held the clock up and regarded it fondly. "Pretty, isn't it? It belonged to my mother. If the movers break it I swear I'll butcher them."

Blimey, Miss Sanderson thought dismally, that's all I need. Well, on with the detecting. "Could you tell me what you remember about that day?"

"*That* day." Setting aside the clock, Nurse Ines took a chair near her visitor. "Rather divides one's life. Certain things happened before, other things after. Well, Miss Sanders, there was nothing outstanding about that day. As usual I went to work even though I was quite ill. I had a bad chest cold but I'm not a shirker and I work no matter how I feel. Mrs. Foster complained I'd given the cold to her baby but I certainly was not near the little thing." She paused and then asked, "Do you want the day in detail?"

"Please."

"I fail to see what bearing this has on anything but here goes." She took a deep breath. "I always arrived at nine sharp and I did that morning. Mrs. Foster wouldn't trust me with a key to the surgery door and so I was required to go to the front door. Mrs. Toogood admitted me and told me her 'missus' was sleeping in because the older boy's birthday was the next day and Mrs. Foster wasn't feeling well. Pregnant again. That woman was like a rabbit, one baby after the other. So I went directly to my desk and took some appointments by the telephone and brought records up to date. Oh, yes, I made up some billing notices too. People ask help freely but don't pay very promptly at times. From eight until eleven the doctor made rounds at Lambert General. He was usually back around twelve and had lunch with his family. I had my lunch and as was my custom ate it at my desk."

"You didn't take luncheon with the family?"

"I told you I stayed as clear of them as I could. I always brought my own. I wouldn't eat food from *her* table anyway. Surgery hours were from one until five. Will you want the names of the patients?"

Miss Sanderson had no doubt Nurse Ines could recite those names. "No, that's not necessary."

"Mrs. Rourke was the doctor's last patient and she didn't leave until three minutes after five. I saw her out and then I locked the door. Miss Sanders, I *know* my job and locking that door was part of it. But that cousin of yours always checked it. She didn't trust me."

"Did she check it that day?"

"She did. I didn't speak to her and she ignored me. Swept in like a duchess, rattled the knob, and swept out again. *Silly*. All the doors in the house lock automatically when they're firmly closed. Then the doctor came out of his office and told me I'd better get home and look after my cold. He said he would clean up. I always tidied the waiting room and examination room before I left. Checked the supply cabinet and cleaned the sink and bathroom and emptied the ashtrays. I never was able to understand why the doctor tolerated patients smoking in the surgery. Filthy habit and so dangerous to the health."

Miss Sanderson had been taking her cigarette package from her purse. She hastily pushed it back but Nurse Ines said tartly, "Now, *you* should know better than that. Smoking leads to heart problems."

"I don't believe that has been conclusively proven," Miss Sanderson said weakly.

"You take *my* word, it does. You're digging your own grave with those disgusting things."

"I thought one dug one's grave with a fork and knife."

The nurse ran icily professional eyes up and down Miss Sanderson. "I must admit you're not overweight. Quit that filthy habit and you may have a few good years yet."

Thanks a heap, Miss Sanderson thought. Aloud she said meekly, "You were telling me about Paul advising you to go home."

"I didn't argue. I really was feeling dreadful. I cleared my desk and went out to the hall. Mrs. Toogood had been lighting the fire in the living room and she came to the doorway and told me if I waited a few moments she would walk me home. So I hurried to get my cape and boots on before she did—"

"Don't you like Mrs. Toogood?"

Nurse Ines considered briefly. "I don't care for her grooming. She could certainly comb her hair and have a dentist fix that missing tooth but she is a good housekeeper. I have nothing against her but her conversation tired me. Her only topic was her 'missus' and how wonderful that woman was. So I hurried out of the house and down the lane. It had been raining earlier and was turning quite cold. I made a mental note to sprinkle some ashes on the side steps to the surgery the next morning. I warned the doctor countless times about those steps. In frosty weather they ice up and a patient might have had a bad fall. As I reached my gate I saw Mrs. Toogood stepping out on the veranda. When I came in here it was cold and I built the fire up. I couldn't bear to think of food, so I ran a hot tub and made up some lemon and honey. Then I went to bed and fell almost immediately into a deep sleep. At five minutes after twelve the next morning the police came battering at my door to tell me about the murders." She spread blunt fingered hands. "That is all I can tell you, Miss Sanders."

Miss Sanderson's hand had been creeping toward her mouth. She jerked it down. If Nurse Ines caught her drumming her nail against her teeth she would doubtless get a lecture on dental hygiene. "Did Paul clean up the surgery as he promised?"

"The next morning when the police took me in to check the drug cupboard the rooms had been neatened. Not the job I would have done but the ashtrays had been washed, the sink scrubbed out, fresh linen put on the examination table. Yes, the doctor must have done it before he settled down at his desk to look over a new medical textbook that had arrived in the post that morning."

"Was Paul in the habit of remaining in his office after surgery hours?"

"I wouldn't say he made a habit of it but yes, he frequently did stay at his desk reading. It's my opinion he was seeking refuge from those sons of his. Waiting until they were ready for bed before returning to the living quarters." Removing the wire-rimmed glasses, she polished already shining lenses. "Odd, that's the same question one of the officers from London asked me. The nice one—Chief Inspector Kepesake. Clean as a whistle and well groomed. The only fault I could find with that man was his deplorable smoking habit."

"Did you speak to him about it?" Miss Sanderson asked hopefully.

"I most certainly did. Very sensible man. Put his jade holder in his pocket and promised that was the last time he would ever use it." Miss Sanderson was fighting to keep from smiling. When Adam Kepesake had visited Robby's flat on his return from Maddersley he had been making good use of his elaborate cigarette holder. Nurse Ines' look of beaming approval vanished and her mouth quirked with distaste. "The detective sergeant with him was disgusting! The most slovenly creature I ever saw. Brummell was his name. A positive disgrace to a uniform!"

"Detective sergeants don't wear uniforms."

"You know full well what I mean. Now, do you have further questions?"

"Only one. Your neighbor—"

"Mr. Johnston? Sad case. In constant pain."

"I was thinking of Miss Beauchamp."

Nurse Ines' pointed nose wrinkled as though she'd suddenly caught a whiff of cigarette smoke. "I know nothing about Miss Beauchamp. She was the doctor's patient but he made house calls on her."

"She never came to the surgery?"

"Once, only. If you have any questions I suggest you ask *her*." Coming majestically to her feet, the nurse resumed her packing.

"You didn't mention your dismissal to the chief inspector?"

"I told you I hadn't. It has no bearing on the case."

"Why did you tell me?"

Nurse Ines turned her head and light reflected from her glasses. "Because I thought *you* should know. Don't bother trying to grieve for your relatives. They weren't worth it. You're fortunate you never knew them. Both Dr. and Mrs. Foster were selfish and callous and cruel."

Scooping up the carton, she strode from the room.

NINE

"NOW YOU MAKE YOURSELF comfy and I'll get some coffee," Linda Beauchamp said and scurried into the kitchen.

Miss Sanderson eyed the two available chairs, passed the one made of chrome and what looked like burlap sacking, and took the one with a high back and brocade covering. It was an odd sitting room, nearly as stark as Matthew Johnston's. The floor boards were bare and besides the two mismatched chairs there were only a bookcase and a table bearing a portable typewriter and sheafs of paper. But the window was hung with thin cotton curtains and spaced along the mantel were an array of ornaments. These consisted of an ivory elephant, a water glass holding a few dried flowers, and a fine set of Georgian candlesticks. However, as in Nurse Ines' cottage, a fire burned brightly on the grate and sitting before it was a large Siamese cat. It was washing one rich brown ear and it paused with crossed turquoise eyes to stare balefully at the visitor.

Miss Sanderson stared balefully back. She disliked Siamese cats. Generally she disliked people who owned Siamese cats. She wondered whether she would dislike Linda Beauchamp. It was hard to tell. The young woman seemed as odd as her sitting room. Hardly before Miss Sanderson had crossed the threshold Linda had told her rapidly that she was so sorry that she hadn't stopped to speak the day Miss Sanderson had arrived in the village. She said the reason she hadn't spoken was that she had a morbid fear of strangers and that this fear had been diagnosed by Dr. Paul as a lack of confidence because she'd failed at every single thing she'd ever tried. If she failed to complete the book he'd encouraged her to write she knew she would do something dreadful to herself.

Much more of this prattle, Miss Sanderson thought morbidly, and I may do something dreadful myself. She hadn't been allowed to say a word, had merely been plucked from the stoop and deposited in this chair. The only consoling thought was that it wasn't going to be necessary to prod Linda Beauchamp into talking.

The girl returned bearing a tray and unleashing a flood of words. "I see you've met my Mitzi. Isn't she a pretty girl? I do so love cats, don't you? So aloof, you have to work for their affection. Not like dogs. Nasty beasts. They either nip at you or jump up with great muddy paws." She handed her guest a cup of muddy fluid. "Powdered coffee and it won't be good. I'm not a good cook. But Dr. Paul told me I have the soul of an artist and artists aren't expected to cook properly. Do have a cake. They're from Marlow's Bakery and are *very* good. I talk too much, don't I? But that's simply because I'm nervous."

"No need to be nervous of me," Miss Sanderson said as rapidly as her hostess. Contagious, she thought, and slowed her voice to a soothing drawl. "You were Paul's patient."

"Not really his patient. There's nothing *wrong* with me. He acted as my mentor. He simply dropped in and talked.

Almost every day. On his way home after his hospital rounds. Always sat in that chair you're using. I think of it as Paul's chair. Sometimes he had only a few moments, sometimes he could stay longer. But he always came. He saved me, you know."

"No, I didn't know. Saved you from what?"

The deluge of words slowed. "From . . . something awful. Perhaps I was going mad . . . perhaps I was . . . well, going to take my life. When I came to Maddersley I was a perfect wreck. I'd tried teaching in a school for girls but I failed at that too. The headmistress tried to be kind and told me I was too sensitive for the profession but the truth is I *loathe* children. I'm terrified of them. They're such cruel beastly creatures. Even Dr. Paul's sons were cruel. Do you know what they used to call me?" Leaning forward, she whispered, "Miss Linda Top-heavy."

Miss Sanderson had to fight to control her expression. When she'd seen Linda Beauchamp before, the leather coat had disguised her figure. But in tight jeans and an equally tight sweater the woman was grotesque. She had a stick-like build, sparrow legs, no hips, scrawny arms. Her shoulders were frail and appeared to strain forward under the weight of the largest breasts Miss Sanderson had ever seen. Even on a woman with the sturdy build of Nurse Ines those breasts would have been astounding but on this delicate creature . . . She managed to say, "That certainly was unkind, Miss Beauchamp."

"Please. I'm Linda and I'll call you Abigail. That way you won't seem so much of a stranger." One clawlike hand gingerly touched the bulging pink sweater. "I begged Dr. Paul to arrange an operation. It can be done, you know. He told me I must accept them first. But he did promise in time I could have it done. First he wanted me to accept my mother's death and how I felt about her."

"Your mother died?"

"About eight months ago. After I lost my position at the school I went home to her. Mother had a nice house in Kent and she was delighted to have me back. Then, she died."

"And Paul helped you come to grips with the grief?"

"With the joy! The wonderful freedom. And the *guilt*. One should not be happy about a mother's death. But she was a monster! An invalid and she simply *devoured* me. As soon as she was buried I sold the house and looked around for a place to rent." The triangular face lit up and the bulging brown eyes glowed. "Abigail, you aren't drinking your coffee."

One sip of the coffee had been enough. Linda definitely must be an artist. She certainly couldn't make coffee. "Was Paul acting as a psychiatrist to you, Linda?"

"He wanted to send me to a specialist in London but I refused to go. I told him, 'Dr. Paul, you're my salvation. Heal me!' And he was doing it. We talked and gradually I realized I had nothing to feel guilty about. Mother had made me an emotional *cripple*. She'd convinced me I could do nothing *right*. Dr. Paul told me he was certain that I have the makings of a great writer. He said I should write a book about my life, share my experiences with people who may need help." She swept long fair hair from her face and pointed at the typewriter. "My book was coming along so *well*. I would read it to him and he would make suggestions. Then *she* ruined it. She ruined *me*."

Miss Sanderson carefully set her cup down. I've a terrible feeling, she thought, who *she* is. "Gillian?"

"I refuse to say her *name*." Jumping to her feet, Linda

started walking around the bare room. Sparrow legs and thin hips jiggled immense breasts. "Abigail, how can a lovely person like you ever have had a cousin like her?"

"What did she do?"

"Ruined my life!" The girl pulled to a halt on the hearth. She braced an arm on the mantel and rested her chin against it. Her voice was muffled. "Dr. Paul died on a Thursday night. The Monday before, he dropped in here as usual in the morning. I was so happy to see him. I gave him coffee and we sat here by the fire and I had my notes on my lap to discuss with him and then . . . Then he told me that that was the last visit he would be making. At first I thought he was joking. He told me I had two choices, either to go to that specialist or go to his surgery once a week until he left for London, of course. Then he tried to explain. He said his wife had said people were *talking*, they were saying there was something *going on* between us. I told him he couldn't desert me. I *needed* him. He became quite cold and curt. He ordered me to make an appointment with Nurse Ines. Then he walked out."

"Did you go to his surgery?"

"Once. I went the day he was . . . the day they all died. He was still cold and aloof. I looked across the desk at him and I started to cry. I told him it was no good; I couldn't sit in the waiting room with all those people staring and whispering about me. I begged him, Abigail; I got down on my knees and begged him for *help*. He told me not to be silly. *Silly*." As though exhausted she collapsed in the chrome chair. "Why did she do it? She had so much. A wonderful home, children, Dr. Paul. She was so pretty. I have nothing. Why did she *do* it?"

Why had Gillian Foster done it? Miss Sanderson wondered. Taken from this poor wretch the only comfort she'd had. But Linda's question must have been rhetorical because she was racing on. "I came back to this house and I got down on my knees again. I begged God to punish the Fosters, to strike them *down*. To make them *suffer*." The thin shoulders heaved and it looked as though the girl was sobbing. That black stuff around her eyes will run, Miss Sanderson thought; it will streak all over her face. But the girl raised bright dry eyes. "And He did it! He killed them all. Her and Dr. Paul and those awful boys. All *dead*. And I don't feel guilty because it makes me *happy*. I don't feel guilty because of mother *or* the Fosters."

It wasn't easy to frame the question but Miss Sanderson managed. "Did you tell the police this?"

"Of course not," Linda said calmly. "They would have thought me mad. Abigail, do you think me mad?"

"I think," the older woman said carefully, "that you're a sensitive person who's had an unfortunate life. In time I'm sure you'll find what you're looking for. Tell me, Linda, will you finish your book?"

"Yes. For Dr. Paul."

"To please him?"

"To *spite* him. To prove I can do something right. If he's beyond knowing I can prove it to the world, can't I?"

"Yes," Miss Sanderson told her. "You can prove it to the world."

That world looked cold and depressing as Miss Sanderson crossed the stone bridge and trudged along the road leading to Maddersley Hall. It had started to drizzle and moisture clung to her head scarf and woolen coat. She passed two houses. The first was set well back from the road and its windows were shuttered. This had to be the ancestral home of Gillian and Irene Markham. The second was smaller, modern, and the lawn was cluttered with gnomes. Some of the tacky little figures held fishing rods over yellowing grass, others clasped tiny gardening tools. She wasn't surprised to spot a sign with ornate letters telling the passerby that this was the residence of Nettie and Oscar Seton. Having seen Nettie, she conjured up a mental picture of a stout, florid-faced man as her mate.

She had no high hopes about the Hall. If it followed the rest of the village it would be either a small shabby manor or an architectural atrocity. It proved to be a pleasant surprise. The Hall was set in grounds that did full justice to its owner's literary reputation in the gardening field. Even in this bleak season the grounds promised spring and summer beauty. Turf swept down from the house like a rich carpet, flowing around the roots of ancient oaks and chestnuts. Masses of hawthorn and rhododendron followed the curve of the driveway and on the east side of the house a formal rose garden had been planted. It was centered by a charming piece of statuary, three small children clutching marble baskets of fruit and flowers.

The house matched its estate. The main portion looked Elizabethan and the two wings were later additions, possibly Georgian. Ivy clung to rose brick and long windows looked out over the valley. It was huge. How many servants would it take to staff a house this size, Miss Sanderson wondered.

She steered a course toward the gracious entrance and then detoured to inspect a maze that wound along the west wing. She loved mazes and edged along between it and the house. One of the long windows opened and a clear voice called, "How thoughtful of you to come around here instead of forcing me to walk practically miles of hall to the front door. How on earth did you guess I was here?"

"I had no idea. I was taking a look at the maze."

"And a fine specimen it is. In my parents' lifetimes it became badly overgrown but Donnie has put it back in marvelous shape. There's a small garden with a fountain at the center that's worth seeing. If the weather weren't so nasty I'd take you through to it. But do come in, Miss Sanders. You look blue with cold and how did you get so wet?"

Stepping over the sill, Miss Sanderson told the other woman, "I walked out from the village."

"Really? Why didn't you drive?"

"I don't drive."

"You should have told me that yesterday. I would have come in and gotten you. I most certainly will drive you back. Do give me those wet things."

While her hostess attended to her outer garments Miss Sanderson gazed around. She liked the room. It was high and white and had hunting prints dispersed at wide intervals on the walls. The furniture matched the room—old, graceful, highly polished. She selected a chair near the hearth. An electric fire was glowing, the coils cunningly simulating coals.

Against this background Mary Maddersley looked much at home. This was a different woman from the one in baggy tweeds in the tearoom. In a silk shirtwaist dress and high heels she looked taller and slimmer. The shapeless felt hat had concealed a fine head of silvering hair sweeping back in soft wings from a high brow. Her voice was lower but her eyes were still shrewd. "I fear," she said, "I was a bit abrupt yesterday. Dora always seems to bring out my worst side. I had no business prying into your reason for coming to the village."

"It was as well you did. It makes it easier for me to ask for assistance. You still are willing to help?"

"In any way I can." Miss Maddersley tugged at a velvet pull. "We'll chat over tea. Have you made any progress since we met?"

"It would appear any number of villagers had no affection for my cousin or her family. As you mentioned, there were bad feelings between Gillian and the Austins and Marlows. Then there is the vicar. To say nothing of Paddy Rourke and Dora Campbell."

"You're trying to be tactful. You also must have heard about Donnie—" She broke off as a stout woman in a blue uniform wheeled a tea wagon in. "Just leave it, Hester. Thank you."

Watching her hostess lifting dishes from the wagon to a low table, Miss Sanderson said, "As I came up the driveway I was wondering how many servants are necessary to keep a house this size running."

"Far too many. We get by with a cook and a housekeeper. Of course, we only use this wing. The rest of the place is closed off. Now, don't be embarrassed. Tell me what you heard about Donnie."

"I understand your brother is an author and also writes a gardening column."

"True."

"That Gillian once worked for him doing typing and—"

"False. She *tried* to do typing for Donnie. I only use two fingers to type and I'm faster and more accurate than she was. What else?"

Miss Sanderson found she *was* embarrassed. How do you tell this woman that people say her only brother is not right in the head? She accepted a Spode cup and reached for a dainty sandwich. Miss Maddersley chuckled. "Let me put it this way. After I left the tearoom yesterday what did Dora tell you?"

"That your brother isn't right in the head," Miss Sanderson said bluntly.

"A typical Doraism. The woman is much like a dog she once had. I'm happy to say someone had the good sense to poison it. As long as the creature was facing you it fawned and licked at your hand. When your back was turned it proceeded to bite at your ankles."

"Why do you patronize her shop?"

"Certainly not for the cuisine. Kate Rourke at the inn is a splendid cook. But Dora's grandmother was my grandmother's parlor maid. One tends to feel a sense of responsibility. Dora's tearoom is a financial disaster. In the summer she does manage to snare the unwary passing through but in the winter she makes barely enough to pay her rent. Do have another sandwich. I sense, like myself, you enjoy the creature comforts. I suppose with women like us they replace other things we've missed."

"Husbands and children?"

"I was thinking mainly of careers. At one time I was a most ambitious person. I—But I'm getting away from the subject. In all fairness I feel I should briefly tell you about my brother. No, don't object. Since the Fosters' deaths I've had to face the fact that of all the people who had motives my brother had the strongest." She put down her cup and muttered, "Until the killer is found I'll have to live with suspicion."

"What if the killer *is* your brother?"

"Haven't you ever noticed that it's uncertainty that is the hardest to deal with? Once one knows the truth . . . well, that can be faced and handled. First I must tell you Donnie is *not* insane. He's highly nervous and can't stand the slightest stress. Older generations would call his condition melancholia. I call it depression and acute anxiety. The reason for this condition goes back to his childhood."

Miss Maddersley waved a hand. "In this room you will notice there are no family pictures. I couldn't bear my parents' smug faces. Mother and father had what is now known as an 'open' marriage. Years ago a union of this type was considered novel and disgusting. Mother, as a liberated woman far in advance of her time, paid as scant attention to her children as she did to her husband. And father was the same. They went separate ways. Mother flitted from Paris to the Riviera to New York. Father buried himself in African jungles and other primitive places. Their children were left to the mercies of servants.

"I was a tough independent child and it did me little harm. In time I went up to Oxford to take a medical degree." She held up her hands and studied them. "I wanted to be a surgeon and I feel I would have been a skilled one. But it wasn't to be. Donnie was a late child, much younger than I. Because of my parents' behavior I always felt responsible for him. He was high strung and delicate. While I was at Oxford my father made a flying trip home, decided Donnie was too frail to be sent away from home to school, and hired a tutor. He didn't take time to check the man out, to examine the validity of his credentials. The references had been forged and Donnie, at the age of eight, was placed in the hands of a sadist and a pervert."

"Dear God," Miss Sanderson murmured.

"Even He proved to be no help to the boy," Miss Maddersley said grimly. "It was weeks before the other servants summoned up enough courage to alert me. By the time I got here the tutor had fled. It was as well for him he did. If

I'd gotten my hands on him I'd have used one of those."
She pointed toward the wall over the mantel. A number of
antique swords sent sparkles of light back from sharp
blades and polished hilts.

"Did you call in the police?"

"No. Oh, don't bother saying it. I know full well I
should have. But there was the scandal and Donnie. He
simply couldn't have stood up under questioning. I called
for the family physician and he arranged for a psychiatrist.
Donnie was like a little . . . like a wounded animal, hiding
under beds and in closets. He'd been badly abused."

"Sexually molested?"

"Among other things. I immediately sent for my parents.
True to form they didn't bother coming directly home.
They decided to break their trip by dropping into a Latin
American country, one that was having what they called
'civil disturbances.' Both mother and father were intensely
curious people and quite fearless. They decided to go out
and watch the disturbances. They were promptly set upon
and killed." Miss Maddersley smiled. "Funny."

"That your parents were killed?"

"That they died together. Except for conceiving Donnie
and me they avoided each other. Anyway, with their
deaths my career was finished. I left Oxford and came back
to act as guardian, surrogate mother, and keeper for a disturbed child." Picking up the teapot, Miss Maddersley
asked, "More tea or brandy?"

"Brandy."

"Excellent choice." She opened a bow-fronted cabinet
and took out a decanter and matching glasses. They
looked like Waterford.

Miss Sanderson took a sip. In quality the brandy

matched its exquisite container. She lifted the glass, smiled at her companion, and said, "To creature comforts."

"And to my parents who I fervently hope are roasting in hell. Back to Donnie. He improved. In time he came close to what is called normal although I have always failed to see what that word signifies. He showed an interest in and a talent for gardening. I encouraged him. Our lives fell into a pattern. We spent the spring, summer, and early fall here and in winter months went to a villa in Corfu purchased by our mother shortly before her untimely end.

"Many times I've tried to persuade Donnie to rent or sell this huge place and find a smaller one elsewhere. But he regards this house as a refuge. After what happened to him in it I fail to see why but we've kept it on. When . . . if this Foster business is cleared up I'm determined we'll leave. Do some traveling, find another garden for Donnie."

Whether it was the thought or the brandy, there was a change in Miss Maddersley. She was smiling and there was no bitterness in that smile. She splashed more brandy in her glass and held the decanter out. Miss Sanderson shook her head. "Tell me about Gillian."

"Ah yes, the enchanting Gillian. I blame my father for criminal negligence in selecting a tutor and yet I was responsible for bringing Gillian Markham, as she was then, into Donnie's life. And, in her way, the girl did just as good a job on my brother as that perverted monster did." Squaring her shoulders, the woman said crisply, "Donnie was working on a book. I'd been doing his typing and I found it tedious. I couldn't work up any interest in mulching and organic fertilizer and pruning. So I looked around for a typist. I'd heard that Gillian Markham was doing some work for the vicar and keeping books at the Fox and

Crow. I'd known of Gillian since she was a baby. I'd seen
her around the village and she was pretty and bright and
had the reputation of being a kindhearted girl—"

"How old was she at this time?"

"Let me see." Miss Maddersley stroked her blunt chin.
"That was about six months before her marriage. About
twenty-one."

"And your brother?"

"Forty-two. I know what you're thinking. April and De-
cember. But Donnie is—or was—young for his age. Completely unworldly. He'd never had a date with a girl and he
was still much of a boy." Miss Maddersley reached for a
metal box and extracted one of her small black cigars. She
took her time lighting it. "Gillian came here three after-
noons each week. When I saw a sample of her work I was
tempted to let her go but there was a change in Donnie.
For the first time in my memory he was truly *happy*. Simply
glowed. Gillian seemed so good for him. She never talked
a great deal but she listened to him by the hour. To be
truthful, Miss Sanders, I began to have selfish hopes. The
girl seemed genuinely fond of Donnie and I thought there
was a good chance for marriage. There would have been
advantages for her—"

"The title?"

"More than being Lady Maddersley. Our family managed to hold on to a good share of its wealth and she
would have been able to entertain, to travel, to enjoy what
I believe they call the 'good life.' And I'd finally be able to
make a life for myself, a bit late but one never knows."

"But it didn't work out?"

"My dream turned into a nightmare." Getting up
abruptly, she said, "Come with me." She led the way to a

door at the end of the room and flung it open. "My brother's study."

The study was as large and gracious as the sitting room. The walls were lined with bookcases and the books didn't look merely decorative; they looked well handled. There were mullioned windows and directly in front of one was a handsome desk. Near it was a smaller desk with an electric typewriter on its polished top. Clamped on a work table was a small flytier's vise and heaped around it was a litter of feathers and silk. Over the mantel was a Constable.

The room, Miss Sanderson mused, of a solitary man, one depending on books for company, on gardening and fishing for occupations. Miss Maddersley made an imperious gesture and her companion walked around the room. On the large desk, the small one, the mantel, were framed snapshots. In all of them were the same two people—a tall gangly man and a petite, very pretty girl. Despite the backgrounds the poses were the same. The girl smiled an enchanting, dimpled smile at the camera; the man gazed down at her with adoration and wonderment.

"They say," Miss Maddersley said in a husky voice, "a picture is worth a thousand words. What do you see?"

"He was infatuated with Gillian."

"Donnie was obsessed with the girl. She always came out here faithfully. Never missed an afternoon. Then one day she didn't arrive. Donnie waited, getting more and more upset. I was going to ring her up and then I decided against it. I thought it was time for Donnie to take a little responsibility. He sat over there—" A shaking finger pointed at the larger desk. "He said a few words, he shook his head, the receiver dropped from his hand, and then he got up and crept over there—" The finger moved and pointed at a corner behind a high-backed chair. "He crouched over there like an . . . like an injured animal.

"I immediately rang through to the Markham house. Gillian answered. I said, 'What did you say to my brother, Miss Markham?' and she said, very brightly, 'Not Miss Markham. I'm Mrs. Foster. I was married this morning.' I couldn't utter a word and she laughed and said, 'Aren't you going to congratulate me?'" Naked hate twisted Miss Maddersley's face. "I asked her why she had done that to my brother, why she had pretended to love him. She said, so innocently, 'I'm sorry that Donnie got the wrong idea. I do like him but I certainly don't love him.' I told her . . . I said I hoped she would one day suffer as she was making my brother suffer. Then I rang off."

"Yet I understand your brother was Paul Foster's patient and so were you."

Turning her back, the other woman strode from the room and Miss Sanderson followed her. "How to make you understand. Dr. Foster was in practice almost two years before we used his services. Donnie doesn't just direct gardeners; he works with them. He gets cuts and scratches and once had blood poisoning. In the winter he frequently has bouts of bronchitis. Dr. Foster was in the village and he knew his business. And . . . Donnie seemed to want to go to him. Whether he was hoping to catch a glimpse of Gillian I don't know."

"Was he home the night of the murders?"

"No." The older woman sagged back in her chair. "I don't know where Donnie was that evening. It had been a foul day with steady rain. Shortly after tea, around five, the rain stopped and it turned cold. Donnie had been restless all afternoon and he said he was going out for a walk.

He said not to wait dinner for him. When I went to bed he still wasn't home."

"What time was that?"

"Around ten. The following morning when I heard about the murders I went out to a shed he has fixed up at the back. His oilskins were hanging on a peg above his rubber boots. They were damp. I wondered whether he had washed them."

Blood, Miss Sanderson thought, blood sprayed from Paul Foster's wounds. Not from Gillian's or Arthur's or Andrew's; from those bodies there had been little blood.

"Later in the day," Miss Maddersley said dully, "I went up to his room. The jacket he'd been wearing the previous evening had stains on the cuff. They looked like blood. When I asked about it Donnie told me he'd slipped on the ice, grasped at a branch, and gotten a gash on his wrist. He showed it to me."

Compassionately Miss Sanderson regarded the other woman. What a hell she had lived in, still was living in. She said gently, "And you wonder . . ."

"Yes, I wonder. On one hand I can't believe a timid man like my brother could kill four human beings. But thinking of what he's gone through, the way Gillian treated him . . . Miss Sanders, I simply don't know."

"Tell me, why didn't anyone in the village try to help the police? Why didn't *you* tell them about Melanie Marlow and Dora Campbell?"

"Because we all have something to hide. People who live in glass houses simply must not throw stones. If I had mentioned anyone else there's a good chance that person might have hit back—told the police about Gillian and

Donnie. So, we all told the same story—how wonderful the Fosters were."

"A conspiracy of silence?"

"An unspoken agreement. Rather cowardly. Will you tell the police?"

"Yes."

"And they'll come back and root out all our tawdry little secrets."

"Among those secrets is the identity of a mass murderer. When you offered to help, you must have known this is what I would do."

"I did. And I want this finished but . . . I don't want my brother hurt." Miss Maddersley pulled herself from her chair as though she'd suddenly aged. She opened a drawer, burrowed into it, and handed Miss Sanderson an enlarged snapshot. "Donnie. Taken shortly before Gillian came to this house."

Sir Donald stood in his sunbathed rose garden. Behind him were the marble children holding baskets of flowers and fruit. He was wearing a shabby green jacket and wrinkled twill trousers. His face was boyish and painfully sensitive. One hand tenderly touched a yellow rose bud.

"Does he look like a mass murderer?" his sister demanded.

"What does a mass murderer look like?"

Miss Maddersley's shoulders sagged. "I'll drive you home, Miss Sanders."

Miss Sanderson followed the other woman down a series of lofty halls. Shadowy rooms opened from the halls. They were high and stately and the furnishings were shrouded in ghostly dustcovers. The walls were lined with oil paintings. In one a young man in jerkin and feathered cap was brandishing a rapier. He had Sir Donald's slender build and sensitive mouth. In another an elaborate ruff framed the face of a woman who looked much like Mary Maddersley. Her chin was lifted and she looked haughty and imperious.

Miss Sanderson found she was eager to leave the beautiful but deathly quiet home of the Maddersleys.

TEN

WHEN MISS SANDERSON STEPPED into the kitchen she was greeted by a gap-toothed smile from the housekeeper, a gurgle from the direction of the playpen, and the tempting odor of sizzling bacon. "Sit right down, miss," Mrs. Toogood ordered. "Breakfast's nearly ready."

"This is awfully good of you."

"No problem. I was making up little Lucy's and heard you stirring around. Thought I'd cook something up for you. Sure could use some flesh on them bones of yours. Thin as a picked chicken." Swinging around, she inspected Miss Sanderson's trim suit and high-necked blouse. "All dressed up and no place to go."

"I thought I'd take a walk around the village this morning."

"That won't take long."

"Perhaps drop into the Fox and Crow for lunch."

Smacking her lips, the housekeeper cracked eggs into sputtering bacon fat. "Kate Rourke does a nice grill. Should try it."

Mrs. Toogood did a nice breakfast herself. Miss Sanderson's was bacon and eggs and fried bread. Lucy ate her thin gruel with every evidence of delight. She managed to knock the spoon out of Mrs. Toogood's hand and smear gruel over herself and the high chair. Mrs. Toogood good-naturedly mopped the baby off and set her back in the playpen. As Miss Sanderson left the room the housekeeper was spreading rashers of bacon in the skillet. Forbidden fruit, and Irene Markham would be most upset if she knew her housekeeper was devouring her food. She won't find out from me, Miss Sanderson thought as she stepped out on the veranda. She looked out on a cold, rain-drenched morning. Hellish weather.

She loped down the steps and along the walk. By the time she reached the gate she remembered the supposed state of her health and slowed. This being a semi-invalid was becoming a bore. She was approaching the vicarage when she spotted a brightly colored blob in the distance. The blob approached rapidly and became a tall man in a scarlet exercise suit bounding through the pelting rain. One arm rose in salute and he drew to a panting stop.

"Miss Sanders, I presume. Daniel Clay. I've been hoping to catch you for a moment. Are you planning to attend services this Sunday?"

"I've no idea whether I'll be here on Sunday, Dr. Clay."

"In that case perhaps you'll have coffee with me." Taking her arm, he escorted her through massed pines to the manse. "Dreary looking house, isn't it? Built in the days when the vicar usually had a good-sized brood."

Miss Sanderson, whose father had been a vicar, remembered those days. Her parents had had such a large family that when her childless aunt offered to raise a tiny Abigail, that offer had been accepted eagerly. But her family home, although as sprawling and shabby as this one, had been cheerful.

In a gloomy hall her companion paused and bellowed, "Mrs. Gay, we have a guest." He lowered his voice. "Sorry if I startled you, Miss Sanders, but my housekeeper is, as the villagers put it, 'as deaf as a post.'" From the shadowy recesses an ancient woman, clad in a floor-length dress of black bombazine, shuffled. The vicar shouted, "Coffee, Mrs. Gay. Please show Miss Sanders to the library."

The crone beckoned and Miss Sanderson followed her down the hall. A finger silently pointed and Miss Sanderson stepped into a room fully as gloomy as the hall. Shadows crouched in corners and it smelled of old leather, smoke, and the cold ashes heaped on the grate. It was chill and damp. Feeling sympathy for anyone forced to use this room, she wandered around.

This room, like Sir Donald's study, contained two desks but both were large and unpolished. There were no snapshots of Gillian Foster. The only pictures were of a religious nature. Above the mantel was a large oil of the crucifixion. It was garish and rather ghastly.

A voice spoke directly behind her. "This is one house where the interior does full justice to the exterior." Dr. Clay had changed into a tweed suit with leather patches at the elbows and a stem of a pipe protruded from a breast pocket. "I shan't invite you to remove your coat, Miss Sanders. Mrs. Gay hasn't gotten around to lighting a fire and this room feels like Siberia. Sometimes I think I run each morning simply to keep the old blood circulating. But I can offer a chair. Do sit down."

He took his place behind one of the desks and Miss Sanderson dropped into a chair in front of it. Rather like one of his flock, she thought, here to pour out her woes. What did she know about the man facing her? Actually not much. Daniel Clay, widower, forty-four, an early marriage and the death of his young wife through pneumonia. For slightly over ten years the spiritual leader of Maddersley-on-Mead. Also formerly an employer of Gillian Foster. Rather a good-looking man—tall and athletic, a frank open face, thinning corn-colored hair, large glasses like an aviator. She didn't care as much for his voice. It was rich and fruity.

The door creaked open and the crone deposited a tray on the corner of the desk. The vicar shook a rueful head. On the tray were a battered enamel pot, a creamer and a sugar bowl, two mismatched cups, one cracked. He sighed. "At least the coffee is fair. I must admit Mrs. Gay is . . . hem . . . a bit beyond housework or cooking. I do most of it myself. And don't ask, Miss Sanders, why I keep her on. I ask myself that question often enough. I suppose the answer is that I inherited Mrs. Gay when I inherited the vicarage and the poor woman has no other place to go."

He handed her the uncracked cup and she took a cautious sip. The coffee proved to be excellent. Daniel Clay was kindly regarding her. "So your visit is only a brief one?"

"I plan to stay until Lucy's guardian comes for her. It's a trying time."

"For all of us, dear lady. It might be easier for you if you had known your cousins. But past is past and we can only strive to make amends. I suppose you've heard Gillian was once close to me. Yes, I can see from your expression the villagers have been talking."

"I was told that she helped you with office work."

"She tried but actually she was about as good at that as Mrs. Gay is at housekeeping. But I didn't mind her inex-

perience. Gillian was amazingly lovely and she lighted up
this house and my life. I was deeply in love with her."

Amazed at his frankness, Miss Sanderson merely stared.
After a moment he continued. "Her marriage to Dr. Foster
came as a devastating shock. It took me quite a time to
recover from it."

"Gillian didn't tell you about her plans?"

"Not a word. I knew, of course, that she'd met the
young man. The entire village knew Miss Markham had
brought her fiancé to meet her sister. But Gillian kept on
coming in to work in this very room and never gave a hint
of what she planned. Why, a couple of days before they
went to London and were married I jokingly told her when
she became mistress here we would have to make changes.
She smiled—Gillian had a wonderful smile—and said yes,
the trees around the house would have to be cut and new
furniture bought." Behind the aviator glasses his eyes were
bleak. "Mrs. Gay told me about Gillian's marriage at breakfast time. I didn't believe it. I went directly down to the
shops and the villagers were buzzing like a hive of bees
about the news. I still thought some ghastly mistake had
been made. Later that day I went to the Markham house.
Gillian answered the door and right behind her was Paul
Foster. She tried to introduce him—"

"Tried?"

"I fear I reacted like an idiot, Miss Sanders. A jealous
fool. I spun on my heels and walked away from them." He
ran a hand over his thin hair. "It took some time before I
came to my senses."

In that time, she mused, this man of God had preached
a couple of blistering sermons about strumpets. The vicar
wrenched his pipe from his pocket and taking a penknife,
cleaned the bowl. His movements were savage and the

tiny blade jabbed into the bowl as though trying to cut through it. "You did reconcile with my cousin," she prompted.

"The Lord lent me strength and I accepted my loss. I went to Gillian and her husband and humbled myself. They were most gracious. Gillian again attended church and in time Arthur and Andrew came with her. I baptized all three of her children and fully expected to baptize the child she was carrying."

"Did Paul not attend church?"

"Not regularly, but as a medical man his time was limited. The boys went to Sunday school classes. I'd expected Gillian to be a fine mother but she disappointed me. She doted on her children and indulged them too much. Now, if I'd been the father of those boys they would have been disciplined. I received several complaints from their teacher, Mrs. Seton, on their conduct during her classes."

"Did you handle the funeral services for the family?"

"I did. It was my painful duty." He waved a hand toward a velvet-shrouded window. "The Fosters are resting in the Markham plot. I wondered whether Dr. Foster's brother would prefer to have his body interred with his own family but I was instructed to bury him with his wife and children. A wise choice."

"You were Paul's patient?"

"Indeed I was. In fact I was in his surgery the day of the deaths. As is my habit I'd been running that morning and had slipped and twisted an ankle. Luckily no serious damage was done, simply some muscles pulled. Dr. Foster put an elastic bandage on my ankle and gave me some painkillers. Mrs. Gay was also his patient and I took her with me as she had a stomach upset that was worrying."

Miss Sanderson watched the man closely. His face was

composed and his voice unctuous but his hands gave lie to both tone and expression. He was cramming tobacco into the carved bowl as savagely as he'd scraped it. Under that calm exterior, she thought, this man positively seethes with emotion. "What did you think of Paul?"

"He was a skilled physician, far the best I've ever had. I wasn't surprised to learn he was taking a practice in London. A village like this could hardly expect to keep a doctor like he."

"What was your opinion of him as a man?"

"I barely knew him." The vicar lit his pipe and smoke spiraled in blue clouds through the chilly air. "Oh, I heard various rumors about him but I pay no heed to gossip. In a place this small it's wise not to bother with that sort of thing."

"Did you hear about Melanie Marlow?"

"Among other matters, yes."

"What other matters?"

"Surely, dear lady, you know it is unkind to speak ill of the dead."

"If we speak only good I'm afraid we'll never find my cousins' murderer."

"That must be left in the hands of the police."

Miss Sanderson caught the eyes behind the outsize lenses and held them. "I insist you tell me."

"Very well. I understand the doctor was most . . . hem . . . interested in a young lady who works at Lambert General Hospital. She's not a nurse but works in the office there, I believe."

"Interested? Do you mean they were having an affair?"

"That is what I heard. You must keep in mind that gossip can be deceptive. But I believe this . . . hem . . . association was common knowledge in the village."

Like hell it was, Miss Sanderson thought inelegantly. If the villagers had known about it one of them would have told me. She had a suspicion the good vicar had been only too pleased to have had this fact elicited. Her mouth set. "Were you interviewed by the police?"

"By a Detective Sergeant Brummell, yes."

"And did you tell him what you've told me?"

"About the girl at the hospital?"

"And your . . . hem . . . association with Gillian Foster."

Ugly color flooded into his face and his jaw jutted. "I don't care for your tone. My friendship with your cousin was quite innocent and long in the past. You must remember I am a man of God."

"You are also a man."

His hand clenched the pipe stem until his knuckles whitened. But the outburst she'd been trying for successfully was fought down. He said gently, "Dear lady, this whole affair must be terribly upsetting. And with the state of your health I'm certain you're completely unnerved."

"You haven't answered my question," she said doggedly.

"No, I did not tell Sergeant Brummell what I've told you. I didn't lie. I merely answered his questions. Those questions didn't touch on our conversation."

Goading him wasn't going to work, she thought, time for a softer approach. She rubbed her brow and sighed. "I'm sorry if I've been rude, Dr. Clay. You're right and this is all a terrible strain."

He refilled her cup and murmured, "I understand completely. Perhaps it would be best for you to return to your home."

"As soon as I possibly can. Did the sergeant ask about your movements on the evening of the murders?"

"Indeed he did. As I told the good man, only the guilty prepare alibis and flee where none pursueth. I spent the evening in this room, quite alone. As soon as I brought Mrs. Gay back from the surgery I sent her to bed. I cooked dinner and then I worked on notes for a sermon until after ten. My ankle was aching abominably and I swallowed a painkiller and went to bed. I heard or saw nothing that could help the officers."

And that seems to be that, Miss Sanderson thought. She found she was as anxious to leave this dark unkempt house as she had been Maddersley Hall. The vicar didn't press her to stay. He walked her to the front door and stepped out on the porch. With the hand clutching the pipe, he made a wide gesture. "A dying village, dear lady."

"Really?"

"Ah, yes. As soon as they can the young people leave for other places—the cities, I suppose. At one time I conducted weddings and christenings. Now, mainly, my work runs to funerals. I look out over my congregation and each year find it smaller. I see middle-aged faces and those of the elderly."

"Perhaps it would be better for you in another church."

"I have requested that. In the new year I have hopes, God willing, I will be sent to minister to a larger flock. But enough of me. May God go with you, Miss Sanders, and give you strength."

She straightened her shoulders and lifted her chin. "I'm sure we'll all feel better when my cousins' murderer is behind bars."

Light glinted from his glasses as he looked down at her. "Vengeance is mine; I will repay, saith the Lord."

"I'm not looking for vengeance," she told him tartly. "I'm looking for safety."

"Safety from what?"

"A person who killed four times could kill again."

"I hardly think so. The violence is directed against one family."

"Lucy is still alive."

"Ah, but soon she'll be gone with her guardian to a new home. Rest easy, dear lady."

The dear lady, fuming inwardly, made her way past the church and crossed the road. She thought of Daniel Clay's hands as he savagely wielded the penknife and wondered whether that hand had once clasped a knife with a long bloody blade. Her thoughts veered to Lucy and she devotedly hoped the child would soon be taken from that house, from this village. Well, on to the inn and the man with dancing Irish eyes who for frustrated passion had plunged his own hand through a pane of glass.

The saloon bar of the Fox and Crow proved to be a welcome change from the vicar's library and the wet, windswept street. It was warm and smoky and smelled deliciously of beer and food. Granted there was little of ye olde English pub about it but the plastic-covered seats looked comfortable and a battered brass rod that looked like it had been salvaged from the original inn ran along the foot of the bar. Two middle-aged men in farming clothes were playing darts and in a corner Nettie Seton bent over a heaped platter.

Paddy Rourke, in shirt sleeves and a knitted vest, presided behind the gleaming expanse of bar. He smiled expansively as she entered. "Beer or something more substantial, Miss Sanders?"

"Both."

He worked the handle and handed her a stein with a flourish. Artistically battered pewter, she noted with a smile. "Japan?"

"Taiwan. If you're looking for antiques you won't find them here. You also won't find roaches and mildew and leaky plumbing."

"Touché. What's on the lunch menu?"

"Nothing creamed." He leaned over the bar. "Nice greasy grilled food. Kate does a mixed grill to a turn."

"So be it," she told him and carried her beer to a table near one of the fake mullioned windows. Across the street she noticed a lilac curtain fluttering at the tearoom window. Dora Campbell was probably counting the clientele of her rival. Wonder what she will say about me? Miss Sanderson thought. Probably call me that nasty, nosy cousin. Ah, well.

The dart players had finished their game, drained their steins, and thumped them on the bar. Paddy reached for them but one of the men shook a grizzled head. "Nowt more, lad."

"Wife after you again, is she, Tom?"

"Tongue never rests, lad. Thinks a pint leads down the path to damnation." The farmer winked. "Be back before closing time."

As they left Miss Sanderson glanced at Mrs. Seton. The matron's knife and fork were fairly flying. She lifted her head, wiped grease from a puffy chin, and inclined her head a fraction of an inch. Miss Sanderson nodded back and wondered whether it was worthwhile to strike up a conversation. She decided against it.

Paddy delivered a heavy china platter and cutlery wrapped in a paper napkin. "We may not be fancy," he told her, "but we're good."

She took a look at the mixed grill. "You're heavenly."

As she cut into a kidney she thought, so who needs genuine beams and sloping floors and leather? So engrossed was she that it took moments to realize someone was hovering over her table. She looked up into Nettie Seton's fleshy face.

"Terrible weather," the woman informed her.

"Dreadful. Unseasonable."

Mrs. Seton grasped eagerly at this. "Just what I told my husband only this morning. 'Oscar,' I told him, 'this is unseasonal weather. Why, we may well have snow.' Oscar agreed."

Miss Sanderson had a hunch Oscar possibly agreed with anything his wife said. Having exhausted this topic, the woman leaned closer and breathed, "I want to extend our condolences on your recent bereavement."

"Thank you." Miss Sanderson willed her eyes away from the delectable but cooling food.

"I assure you, Miss Sanders, we did all we could to render assistance in that tragic hour. The night it happened Mr. Johnston rang us up and Oscar and me got out of bed and went to his cottage. Irene Markham was in awful shape."

"I can well imagine."

"Having hysterics, she was. The police doctor was trying to give her a shot to calm her and she was fighting him. I had to hold her down. Mr. Johnston, poor man, couldn't help. He was holding the baby and she was squalling her head off. I said maybe she's cold and Mr. Johnston, he put a fold of that tartan rug around her. Then Oscar and me took the poor mite and Irene right home with us." Mrs. Seton paused to catch her breath and then raced on. "Kept them for two days we did. Then Irene tells us she's taking the baby home. Oscar and me begged her to stay on with us or take the wee one to her rooms behind the dress shop but Irene said, 'No, the child is going home.' Took Lucy back to *that* house. Miss Sanders, what do *you* think of that house?"

Hiding her distaste, Miss Sanderson gazed back into the brightly avid eyes. "It seems extremely comfortable."

"It's cursed, you know. Should be burnt to the ground and then sprinkled with salt," Mrs. Seton hissed. She straightened and said in a lofty tone, "If Oscar or I can render any assistance to you and Irene you need only ring us up."

She swept out of the bar and Miss Sanderson sighed with relief. Paddy, smiling broadly, circled the bar and picked up her empty stein. "After that I think you could use a refill." He raised his voice. "Kate, safe to come out now. Nettie's gone."

The door behind the bar opened and a plump woman in a pink dress and flowered apron bustled in. "Draw one for me, me boy." She came directly to Miss Sanderson's table and sat down. "That woman! Talk the ears off a brass monkey." She looked down at Miss Sanderson's platter. "And your lunch all cold. I'll cook more up for you."

"No, thank you, Mrs. Rourke—"

"Kate. Even me boy calls me that."

"I managed to eat a good part of it before she descended on me. What's her Oscar like?"

"Big red-faced buffoon who wouldn't say boo to his wife."

The women exchanged smiles. Kate Rourke may have gained weight with the years but she still had a fresh, blue-eyed prettiness. Paddy came back with three steins and sat down beside his mother. "Cheers."

"Surely," Kate told him, "an Irish lad can make a better toast than that."

"Too long-winded, Kate. By the time the toast is made the beer is flat."

They drank deeply and then Kate Rourke asked, "You'll be staying much longer?"

"Only until Dr. Foster's brother arrives."

"Glad am I that the child is to be his. Irene's a well-meaning woman but knows little of children. Your health is poorly?"

Miss Sanderson touched the lapel of her jacket. "Not too robust."

"And you coming down at a time like this. For the baby's sake it's a kind idea. For your cousin and her husband . . . they were gobshites."

"*Kate,*" her son chided.

"Only truth passes my lips."

"And your tongue outraces your brain."

Irish eyes locked and Kate tossed her glossy dark curls. "Miss Sanders, will you be telling this boy the truth? Four days since you've come and I know you've heard worse than I just said."

"Gillian and Paul certainly didn't seem popular, Kate."

"See. She knows," Kate told her son. "Almost ruined my lad's life did that cousin of yours. With her lying tongue and her false pretty smiles. And me, taken in as surely as my Paddy was. Starting to count my grandchildren I was and then that Jezebel married her fine doctor. Then to find she'd led astray not only us but Sir Donald and the vicar."

"You didn't have any idea about the other two men? Surely in a place this size . . ."

Kate held up her stein and Paddy took it and his own to the bar. His mother ranted, "Gillian Markham had the face of an angel. She smiled and dimpled and led us astray. I could have sworn on the Good Book she loved my boy. And all the time Sir Donald and the vicar thought the same. I well remember the morning Alfred Austin came in for his pint and told us the hussy was wed. My Paddy reached right across the bar and picked the little man up and shook him like a rat. He thought Alfred was lying about his girl. But it was the truth. When we finally believed, Paddy walked over there and drove his fist through that window. See, these scars on his hand." Paddy was putting down the steins and his mother grabbed one of his hands and held it up. On the back of it was a network of fine white scars. "The good Lord was merciful and the cuts were shallow. Soon's I bound them up he took a bottle of whiskey and went to his room and drank himself senseless."

While his mother applied herself to her beer, her son said gravely, "I seldom touch spirits, Miss Sanders. Content myself with a pint now and again. But how I loved that girl . . ."

"And yet you were Paul Foster's patient."

"I was. Kate and me both. He was a good doctor and handy. And Gillian was no longer my girl. She was his wife and she had babies—"

"Who should have been my grandchildren," his mother said brokenly.

"Hush, you'll get your grandchildren." He looked earnestly at Miss Sanderson. "Maybe love wears out. Gillian was another man's wife. She bore his children. Can you understand?"

Miss Sanderson nodded but she asked herself, does hate wear out? "When did you last see Gillian?" she asked the innkeeper.

"I remember well the day. I'd fallen bringing up a keg from the cellar and my chest was paining. Rog Austin took me up to the Markham house in his van. Gillian was on the veranda with her sons. She said, 'Paddy, you're hurt!' She was wearing a coat the blue of her eyes and a white fur hat. Her face was so rosy and pretty framed in white fur."

"Only skin deep was that beauty," his mother rasped. "My Paddy had cracked two ribs."

"How long was that before . . ."

"A week," Paddy said. "But Kate was in the surgery the day they were killed."

"Change of life," Kate said. "Hot and cold flashes. Dr. Foster gave me a prescription for hormones. Helped some."

Miss Sanderson turned to the man. "The evening of the murders, I suppose you were here in the bar."

A smile with no mirth displayed fine white teeth. "No alibi for that evening, Miss Sanders. As I told the chief inspector who questioned us, I was up in bed. Kate was handling the bar. Slow night anyway."

"Your ribs?"

"They weren't troubling me. I had taken a chill and Kate told me to get to bed. I went upstairs about four in the afternoon. And to get out of the inn I had only to drop out of my window onto the roof of a shed and no one the wiser." He touched his chest. "Number one suspect. The motive and the opportunity."

"Don't joke about it, Paddy," his mother muttered. She lifted a defiant chin. "My Paddy could never harm a woman or children."

"What about a man?" her son asked.

His mother's mouth snapped open but at that moment the door opened, bringing in a gust of cold moist air and the elderly couple Miss Sanderson had seen in the lilac-and-lavender tearoom.

Paddy was on his feet. "You'll be wanting a toddy to warm you."

"And a meat pie," the man said.

"Beef," the old lady told Kate.

Nodding cheerfully at Miss Sanderson, Kate headed toward her kitchen.

As Miss Sanderson trudged through the rain up the slope to the pasture she mulled over the days she had spent in this village. Chief Inspector Kepesake had been correct about the villagers talking to a relative of the Fosters. I'm fairly adept at digging up information, she told herself, but no damn good at putting it together. That has always been Robby's work, not mine. And it's a job at which he's extremely talented. I've gone as far as I can go, she admitted, time to call the experts in.

When Mrs. Toogood admitted her to the Markham house, Miss Sanderson glanced at her watch and sat down on the telephone chair. Lifting the scarlet phone, she dialed a familiar number. The housekeeper made no move to leave the hall but Miss Sanderson didn't mind. Arrangements had been made to cover eavesdroppers. Regular cloak and dagger, she thought wryly.

In Robby's chambers at the Temple the receiver was lifted and Mrs. Sutter's crisp voice repeated the number just dialed. "Abigail Sanders, nurse. I'd like an appointment with Dr. Forbes."

"One moment, Miss Sanders, and I'll check with doctor."

As she waited she glanced in the mirror opposite. She admitted she looked as though she could use the services of a physician. Her austere face was thinner, there were indentations under her cheekbones, faint hollows in her temples, and the clear blue eyes were circled by dark smudges that resembled the eye makeup Linda Beauchamp used with such a lavish hand. Nothing like a few days in a quiet village . . .

Mrs. Sutter's voice crackled in her ear. "Doctor is able to work you in early tomorrow, Miss Sanders. Shall we say nine A.M. Will that be convenient?"

"That will be fine."

"Doctor suggests you come to the city today if possible. He'll want tests and you know how tiring they can be. He suggests you have a good rest tonight so you'll be fresh in the morning."

"One moment." Miss Sanderson looked up at the housekeeper. "Are there any buses to London this afternoon?"

"One at two." Mrs. Toogood consulted her watch. "If you hurry you can make it. I'll help."

Miss Sanderson told Mrs. Sutter she would be leaving the village at two. As she put down the telephone, she said, "I'm going to have to rush."

"I'll get your bag packed." Mrs. Toogood was on her way up the stairs. "You sit and rest. Poor lamb, you do look peaky. You won't have to lug that big case. I'll stick a few things in the missus' overnight bag."

"I'll need—"

"I know what you need."

In a remarkably short time Mrs. Toogood was back and handed the other woman a small leather case. "Now, don't you run, hear? Time enough to get to the bus. Stops right in front of the inn. I'll tell Miss Irene." Removing the chain, she opened the door. "You'll be coming back, miss?"

"I'll be back," Miss Sanderson promised.

She forced herself not to break into a run. She passed the houses on Jericho Lane and trotted down the hill. The bus was already drawn up in front of the Fox and Crow. Near it Paddy Rourke was talking to Alfred Austin. As Miss Sanderson drew level with the chemist's the doors of the bus closed and she broke into a run, waving frantically. Paddy grinned and thumped on the bus door. It swished open and Paddy grasped her arm and helped her up the steps. "Where are you off to in such a rush?"

"To see my physician."

"Keep moving at that pace and you'll need the man." He stepped back and called, "Walk soft, Miss Sanders."

She paid the fare and sank on a seat. This acting the role of an invalid was debilitating. She actually *was* short of breath. Glancing around at the other passengers, she saw no familiar face. She opened her handbag, took out a small journal and a pen, and proceeded to bring her notes up-to-date. Each evening, upon retiring to the guest room in the Markham house, she'd filled out the events and conversations of the day. Too bad she hadn't dared use the large handbag fitted with a miniature tape recorder that she had on other cases. But it would have been too risky.

When her notes on Dr. Clay, Nettie Seton, and the Rourkes had been faithfully recorded she tucked the journal away and rested her head against the seat back. I'll close my eyes for a moment, she thought.

She slept all the way to London.

ELEVEN

ROBERT FORSYTHE UNLOCKED THE door of his flat and Miss Sanderson, with a sense of homecoming, stepped into the foyer. This place as well as his family home in Sussex were as familiar to her as her own flat. She took off her coat and muffler and hung them on the brass knobs of an old-fashioned clothes tree. This and many of the other furnishings had been brought up from Sussex. They fitted in well with the high ceilings and spacious rooms of his London home. While he carried her case into the guest room where she had spent countless nights she wandered into the sitting room and switched on table lamps.

When he joined her she handed him the journal. "The product of four hellish days and three nights that were worse. Adam Kepesake had better be grateful. There're enough suspects in there to satisfy even him. Would you like to read it?"

"We'll discuss it later, Sandy. Right now we're going to dine in high style. You rest—"

"Robby! That word makes me furious. I've heard it ad nauseam."

"From the looks of you I'm not surprised. You've lost pounds. Never mind, this dinner will put weight back on."

"Not if you cooked it."

He held up a hand and smiled. "Hardly back and insulting me already. And I didn't cook it. I rang up Raoul—"

"Lionne d'Or?"

"Yes. And I told Raoul I was entertaining a special lady, so he sent dinner around."

"What's on the menu?"

"Haven't the foggiest. Everything's in hot boxes or cold ones. And a basket of wines." He walked across the Bokhara carpet toward the hall. "We'll soon know."

While she waited she wandered around the room. She touched the corner of a Queen Anne table that once had graced the drawing room of the Sussex house and paused beside the glass case. Sir Amyas' Buddha was the largest figure and the one that had spurred Robby into this hobby. She lifted the glass and fingered a tiny Fu dog carved from pink jade. She'd given this to Robby on his birthday and still winced at the price.

"Madame, dinner is served," Forsythe called from the doorway.

She regarded him affectionately. Even in his pose as maitre d' with his long head humbly bent and a linen napkin draped over one wrist he looked elegant. She ruffled his fine hair and brushed a kiss across his cheek. "What's this all about?" he asked. "You generally aren't demonstrative."

"I may be getting senile but I find I've missed you and even those cramped ancient chambers."

"Damp spots and smoking hearths and all?"

"Even those. Let's eat!"

They dined by candlelight at a table with fine linen,

china, sparkling silver, and a centerpiece of pink roses. After a time Miss Sanderson looked up from her smoked trout, took a sip of superb Chablis, and said, "My compliments to the chef. As Mrs. Toogood would say, Robby, you've done this up brown."

"No shop talk. Enjoy."

She enjoyed course after delicious course. As she scooped up the last fragment of Tournedos Rossini, she moaned. "Blimey, I'm stuffed! I can't eat another bite."

"Not even mousse?"

"Chocolate?"

"Blueberry."

She was tempted but she shook her head. "Perhaps as a bedtime snack. I think you're right and I just put weight back on."

"Good. Amuse yourself while I haul this stuff into the kitchen."

"I'll help."

"Not necessary, Sandy. One advantage of a service flat is a good fairy called Mrs. Tupper who will put all in order in the morning."

Returning to the sitting room she gazed indecisively at the hearth. All was prepared for the touch of a match. The room was pleasantly warm and there was no necessity for a fire but she snapped her lighter and watched the kindling catch. Then she stooped and laid a chunk of wood on the small blaze. Forsythe touched her shoulder and she jumped. "Nervy, aren't you? And also using up the logs Meeks faithfully brings up from Sussex."

She perched on an armchair, the one Adam Kepesake had used the last time she'd been in this room. "There's something about an open fire that central heating can't compete with."

"Touches a memory of remote ancestors crouching around a blaze. Appeals to something primal in all of us."

"Warding off an evil that lurks just beyond the ring of firelight."

Forsythe gave her an intent look. "Methinks I have a quotation that sums up your frame of mind. It goes—"

"Please, Robby!" She lifted a protesting hand. "Don't spoil Raoul's masterpiece with *Macbeth*."

"In this case I think Coleridge said it better."

> *Like one that on a lonesome road*
> *Doth walk in fear and dread,*
> *And having once turned round walks on,*
> *And turns no more his head;*
> *Because he knows a frightful fiend*
> *Doth close behind him tread.*

Miss Sanderson repeated, "'Doth close behind him tread.' That does sum it up. That's exactly my reaction to the little village of Maddersley-on-Mead."

"And you haven't been sleeping well."

"Understatement. I've hardly been sleeping at all. By evening I was exhausted and yet when I was in bed I merely dozed. You know the creaks and groans in a house. I'd swear every time a timber creaked I'd sit bolt upright. And I went into the nursery any number of times every night to stand over Lucy's crib and make sure she was safe." She gave a shaky laugh. "I think I'm losing my grip."

"Not much wonder, Sandy. But there's an answer." He tapped the journal with a long finger. "You've done your job. Ring Miss Markham in the morning and inform her your physician refuses to allow you to return."

"Not to return would be cowardly. And don't give me that quotation about living to fight another day. I am *not* leaving that child in that cursed house."

He lifted his brows. "Cursed? More of your fey feelings?"

"Recorded fact. Three previous murders in the Markham house. All using a knife." She pointed at the journal. "Read it."

"I'd rather you tell me about it. And about everything else you've seen and heard."

She glanced at the mantel clock. "It will take hours."

"Not as long as you may think. Beau Brummell gave me duplicates of the material you had. I've studied the layout of the village and the plan of the house as well as the names and data on the residents. That should help. But you'd better start talking. On the stroke of midnight, finished or not, you're off to bed."

Settling back against the cushions, she started to talk. She began her account when she'd stepped down from the bus in front of the Fox and Crow. Robert Forsythe sat as quietly as she did, his eyes on her face.

"—and so I got on the bus and left Maddersley this afternoon." She took a deep breath and rubbed her throat. "Half past eleven. Not bad, Robby."

"Excellent! Sandy, you've a mind like a computer."

"At times I wish I had the emotions of one." He busied himself at the liquor cabinet and handed her a glass. She had no need to wonder whether this one was Waterford. It was. She took a sip and beamed. "Your best and oldest brandy. Now, have you any sparkling ideas?"

"Not as yet. This will take some mental digesting." He shook his head. "But this explodes the idea of Happy Family, doesn't it? It appears the Fosters were not wonderful people beloved by all."

"Hardly. You can practically cut the hate with a knife—"
She laughed. "I wish I hadn't used *that* word."

"Have you any favorite candidates for murderer?"

"Practically any person mentioned in the journal. And not an alibi among them."

"The exceptions?"

"Mary Maddersley."

"Why?"

"From the moment we met in the tearoom she knew I wasn't there solely to support Irene. Miss Maddersley was aware I was searching for the killer and yet she volunteered all that information about her brother and told about others who had reason to hate the Fosters."

"She sounds intelligent."

"She is."

"Have you considered Mary Maddersley could be using a clever ploy. Throwing you off her own scent by dragging red herrings along before your quivering nose. She had as good a motive as Donald Maddersley and the opportunity to commit the murders."

"I still don't think—"

"Anyone else?"

"Matthew Johnston. No motive. And he had everything to lose by his neighbors' deaths."

"Hmm." Forsythe templed his fingers and gazed down at them. "Gillian Foster was famous or perhaps infamous for toying with people's emotions. Suppose she'd tired of playing wonderful neighbor to the old chap and had tried to discard him? She had played that dangerous game with many others."

"True. The job she did on Melanie and her parents was heartless and cruel. To say nothing about Linda Beauchamp and Nurse Ines and—"

"How about the three men she led down the garden path?"

"Right. But Matthew was in the house the afternoon of the murders. Not only did Gillian welcome his help but she welcomed *him*. When the Fosters moved to London they planned to have him visit. And, Robby, Matthew adored Gillian."

Forsythe shrugged. "Not one of my better suggestions. And now, Cinderella, off to the guest room."

"I still have ten minutes before midnight."

"Which will be put to good use by showing you your props."

"Don't tell me you're sending me back in a false mustache."

"Come along and see." He led the way down the hall to a comfortable guest room. Opening the wardrobe, he pulled out a shopping bag. *"Voilà!"*

"Blimey. Harrods, no less."

"If a well-to-do lady like Miss Abigail Sanders has time to put in in London town, where does she head? To Harrods, of course. Incidently, Mrs. Sutter took this chore on. Let's see what we have." He emptied the bag on the bedspread. "A pattern book of sweaters for tots and knitting needles and wool. You can knit, can't you?"

"Of course." Miss Sanderson fingered pale green wool and white angora. "This would look sweet on little Lucy." She picked up a jar. "I've excellent taste in caviar. Beluga!"

"And in whiskey." He handed her a squat brown bottle.

"What's this thing?"

"Obviously a book. Quite a tome."

"All about the Tudor dynasty. Robby, I never read history."

"But Mrs. Sutter is a history buff. No doubt hoping you'll pass it along to her."

Handing him the book, she repacked the bag. "You can pass it on. I'm not lugging that heavy thing around. What's that? More props?"

He handed her a folded paper. "Prescriptions from old Dr. Forbes."

Her eyes widened. "Does he really exist?"

"He's a police surgeon. We decided on some heart medicine and something for blood pressure—"

"Exactly the ailments I dreamed up, Robby. What about my thyroid condition?"

He chuckled. "Sandy, your power of invention exceeds ours. You're to have the chemist in Maddersley fill these prescriptions and then you are to promptly flush them down the loo." He paused and cocked his head. The mantel clock was booming out Westminster chimes. "The witching hour. Into bed." Putting his hands on her shoulders, he dropped a light kiss on her brow. "Tonight you will sleep soundly, Sandy."

"Is that an order?"

"It is."

"Then clear out so I can obey."

Miss Sanderson was barely under the eiderdown before she obeyed. Sleep came down in soft, comforting waves and, happily, was dreamless.

TWELVE

FORSYTHE HAD BEEN IN the office at New Scotland Yard long enough for the watery morning sunlight, which had merely touched the window pane when he had arrived, to be streaming into the room and settling in a pool on the carpet at his feet.

Behind a desk that was graced by a handsome silver and ebony desk set Chief Inspector Kepesake bent his head over Miss Sanderson's journal. To his right his sergeant, looking like something the cleaners had neglected to remove, lounged in an armchair. Brummell did look out of place in the luxurious surroundings provided by Kepesake but Forsythe noted the man had worked through the journal at twice the speed of his superior. I must stop having these niggling thoughts about Kepesake, Forsythe told himself sternly. Despite his foppishness he really is quite a competent officer.

Kepesake grimaced and muttered, "Miss Sanderson certainly put every detail in. Even Nurse Ines' remarks about my smoking."

The barrister looked pointedly at the cigarette smoldering in the jade holder and Kepesake said quickly, "I am contemplating giving up smoking. Nurse Ines is right; it's a filthy habit. Why only last week I burnt a hole in my favorite vest."

Forsythe grinned and Brummell winked at him. Closing the journal's cover, Kepesake sat back in his chair. "I don't think there's any argument about our wisdom in sending Miss Sanderson to Maddersley-on-Mead. In a short time she's managed to ferret out information from the villagers that we didn't get in two weeks."

"At a price," Forsythe told him curtly. "Sandy's face looks like a death's head and she's so jumpy it's distressing."

Brummell tapped his own notebook. "She's given us a number of leads."

"Which we will follow up immediately," Kepesake told him. "Directly after lunch we'll go back to that village and this time those people are going to think they're perched on that grill at the Fox and Crow that Miss Sanderson keeps mentioning."

"You most definitely will *not*," Forsythe rasped. "You'll wait until Sandy is out of there. You owe her that much."

Brummell said quickly, "Chief, those folks will guess where our tips came from."

"So? I don't imagine Miss Sanderson will mind a little displeasure from the locals."

Forsythe came half out of his chair but Brummell waved him back. "The chief hasn't thought it out, Mr. Forsythe. It could be dangerous for the lady, Chief."

"In what way?"

"The killer might figure she knows more than she does. Might get the wind up and go after her."

"I'll admit that hadn't occurred to me. No, we can't endanger her. Very well, Beau, we'll leave it until Monday. By that time she'll be out—"

"What do you mean?" Forsythe demanded.

Fitting a fresh cigarette into his holder, Kepesake said, "Shortly before you arrived we heard from Leonard Foster. His wife and he will be back in London on Sunday—"

"The day after tomorrow."

"That's right, old boy. So you can rest easy. I told Mr. Foster about Miss Sanderson and he was most gratified she's been watching over his little niece. He promised he'd bring Miss Sanderson back with them when they pick up Lucy Foster."

"Only two more days," Forsythe muttered.

The chief inspector flicked an ebony and silver lighter and exhaled a cloud of smoke. "I still don't understand why your secretary insisted on going back to that place. Her work was finished."

"Not quite. There's the baby. Anyway, Sandy is like a bulldog. Once she gets her teeth in it's impossible to make her let go." Forsythe glared across the desk. "And you're the one who got her into this mess."

"Not the chief," Brummell said soothingly. "As I told you, it was all my idea."

"And an excellent one, Beau." Kepesake pointed at his sergeant's notebook. "Do you have the names of all the suspects jotted down?"

"Every last one. Makes quite a list."

"We'll tackle the likely one first."

"Who's that, Chief?"

"That Maddersley chap. It's obvious he's dreadfully unstable."

Pulling out his pipe, Forsythe tamped fragrant tobacco

into its carved bowl. "That applies to Linda Beauchamp as well."

Kepesake waved smoke and the suggestion away. "Old boy, stabbing is traditionally the crime of a male."

"No more than poisoning is a woman's crime," the barrister said drily.

"I still like Maddersley." Kepesake turned to his sergeant. "We'll leave Doctor Clay until last."

"Why, Chief?"

"You interviewed him. Can you picture that man murdering four members of his congregation?"

Rumpling his shaggy hair, his sergeant said mildly, "He's a powerful chap, Chief, and has a strong motive and no alibi."

"Nonsense! Daniel Clay is a *minister*."

"So was the man who killed two of his choirboys and dismembered their bodies in Essex last fall."

"Nonetheless at present I happen to like Maddersley. What a headline that would make! *Baronet Butchers Doctor's Family*."

It's no use, Forsythe thought, I really can't *stand* this ass. Aloud he said, "I'd keep Miss Markham in mind too."

"We'll do a thorough job, Forsythe. None of them will be neglected. Not even that dowdy woman who has the tearoom. Lavender and lilac!" Kepesake gave a delicate shudder.

Glancing from his superior to Forsythe's set face, the sergeant said quickly, "'Bout this list you gave us to run down, sir—"

"Yes, that list," Kepesake said testily. "Forsythe, so you think we simply sit on our hands and let private detectives like you do our—"

"I am *not* a private detective."

Again Brummell interceded. "What the chief is getting at, sir, is we've already checked out both matters. When we found Melanie Marlow had been the Fosters' servant and had left the village recently we ran her down. Didn't know then about her father going after the Fosters but we figured maybe she could tell us something."

"Is she taking a hairdressing course?"

Brummell grinned. "Not so's you would notice. Melanie's an attractive girl in a flashy way but as cheap and hard as they come. Located her in one of those places making porno films for clubs and rundown cinemas in the East End. When I interviewed her she was wearing high heels and a string of beads and that's about all. Didn't seem to bother her a bit."

"Good Lord! She's only a child. Not seventeen yet."

"Know that, sir. We've taken steps and Melanie's gone into early retirement. At least from the film business. Slimy character who was kind of the director swore she'd claimed to be over twenty. Looks that old too."

"I've known many girls like her," Kepesake said philosophically. "Generally end up as prostitutes."

Ignoring him, Forsythe asked Brummell, "Could she tell you anything?"

"Not much. Didn't let on about her parents not knowing her whereabouts but she did gabble on about the Fosters. Boasted the doctor was wild about her and had his hands on her all the time. Said he'd promised to come up and see her in London." Brummell's wide jaw set. "If she were my daughter I would take a belt to her and then buy a chastity belt."

"If she were your daughter, Beau, there would be no problem," the chief inspector told him expansively. "Bad blood, I've seen many girls like—"

"And that's all she said?" Forsythe asked the sergeant.

"That's about it. Oh, she carped about the boys, said they were brats. Made a lot of snide remarks about Mrs. Foster. Called her a jealous bitch and claimed Mrs. Foster paid her off to get her out of the house." Brummell looked down at the short list Forsythe had made. "This item about Miss Beauchamp, sir. No, she's never been in a mental institution. I rang up the headmistress of the school where she'd worked and the woman told me Miss Beauchamp simply couldn't handle the girls. She was afraid of them and they knew it and made her life hell."

"And Miss Beauchamp's mother?"

"Mrs. Beauchamp had arthritis, the crippling kind. But she died from an embolism. Died in the hospital and there's no way her daughter could have had a hand in her death."

Kepesake waved his jade holder. "Which ruins your idea, old boy, of the young woman being involved with a previous murder."

The barrister continued to ignore him. He sat quietly, his neglected pipe in hand, his eyes fixed on a point beyond Brummell's shoulder. The sergeant watched him with bright hopeful eyes. "You thought of something, sir?"

"A few words," Forsythe said slowly. "Words that don't fit. As you know Sandy has a remarkable memory. She can repeat entire conversations word for word. Last night I didn't catch this but after I put her on the bus this morning I checked it in her journal. It may be nothing . . ."

"Tell us about it sir," Brummell urged.

Forsythe told him. The chief inspector listened as intently as his sergeant. When Forsythe was through, Kepesake ran a hand over his perfectly styled hair and said dubiously, "That's going to present some difficulty. Beau?"

"Well, I don't know, Chief . . ."

"We'll give it our best," Kepesake said decisively. "That's a remarkable secretary you have, old boy."

Getting to his feet, Forsythe looked down at the other man with hard eyes. "I'm well aware of that and I want her back. I want Sandy back soon and unharmed. If anything should happen to her, *old boy*, you will answer to me."

As Forsythe was leaving New Scotland Yard his secretary climbed down from the bus in front of the Fox and Crow. She shifted the shopping bag to her left hand and picked up the overnight case with her right.

She was struck with a sensation of *déjà vu*. When she'd left London the sun had been shining but the sky over Maddersley-on-Mead was as sullen and gray as it had been the day of her arrival in the village. Behind her the shops huddled drearily and directly in front was the facade of the inn. To complete her feeling the brass-bound door swung open and Paddy Rourke, wearing a wide smile, strolled toward her. At his heels a small terrier trotted stiffly. Its muzzle was white with age.

"Back again, are you?" Paddy said jovially. "And you've been spending your money in the fancy shops."

"I did a bit of shopping. Nice dog." She bent to stroke the animal. "What's his name?"

"Sammy." Scooping up the terrier, he nuzzled his chin against its grizzled head. "And I fear he's not much longer for this world. Gone downhill since we lost Sally. Litter mates they were and Sammy took it hard."

"Sally died?"

"Poisoned! Some cowardly gobshite—" He broke off and his Irish eyes shone with tears. "What kind of fiend would poison a harmless old beastie like Sally?"

The same fiend Coleridge had written about in his poem, Miss Sanderson thought as she shook her head. The innkeeper blinked his tears away. "But I'm forgetting, Miss Sanders. Irene Markham's inside having a bite of lunch and asked me to step out and tell you to join her. Your bag—"

"No. It's light, Paddy."

He held the door for her and she stepped into the warmth of the saloon bar. The Fox and Crow was doing a rushing business. Only two tables were unoccupied and a drone of voices competed with the blare of the television turned to a soccer game. She made her way to the bar and Paddy drew a pint for her. "Market day," he told her, "and the lads are wetting their whistles before driving to Lambert. Will you be wanting a bite?"

"I think not. I had rather a large breakfast."

"There's your cousin, then, waving to you."

She circled a table surrounded by men clad in rough clothes and smelling pungently of their barns. Irene sat alone by a window. On the table was a pewter stein and a plate containing half a ham roll. Setting her case and the bag on one chair, Miss Sanderson sank down into another. "Sorry to run off like that, Irene. I didn't have time to write a note."

"Are you all right? What did your doctor—"

"The tests aren't completed as yet," Miss Sanderson lied. "But not to worry. Simply a precaution."

Her reassurance wasn't really necessary. Irene didn't seem all that concerned. Her color was high and there was a sparkle in the milky blue eyes. Flinging back short hair, she blurted, "I heard from him. This morning. He rang up and—"

"Who?"

"Leonard Foster, that's who. Marjorie and he will be

back this Sunday. Told me, just like that, they'll expect Lucy to be ready. Even asked me to drive to Heathrow and pick them up. The nerve!"

Miss Sanderson sagged with relief. Sunday! Only another forty-eight hours and she would be free to leave. Fervently she hoped never to see this village again. Irene was staring at her and she managed to ask, "Are you going?"

Nibbling at the roll, Irene said, "I was tempted to tell Leonard to get here any way he damn well could. Then I reconsidered. I haven't been out of this village for months. I feel . . . oh, I don't know."

"Stifled?"

"Yes. As though I should see something beside The Cheese Tease and Ferne's Market." She regarded the Harrods bag with envy. "Do some shopping, perhaps go to the theater and have dinner with one of the women I once worked with. Do you understand?"

"Completely."

"Good. I want to request a favor, rather a large one. That is, if you feel well enough to—"

"I'm fine. What is it, Irene?"

"I'd like to drive to London tomorrow and have the day there. I've spoken to Mrs. Toogood and she's willing to stay with you tomorrow and remain the night. She'll be in the house until the Fosters and I arrive on Sunday. I know it's an imposition but—"

"I'd be happy to." Reaching over, Miss Sanderson patted Irene's hand. "A change will do you good."

The younger woman beamed. "I knew I could count on you. Perhaps I haven't told you but I do so appreciate all you've done. It's so comforting to have a cousin to rely on. And we'll keep in touch from now on, won't we?"

Feeling incredibly false, Miss Sanderson nodded. She took a sip of bitters and asked, "You're serious about keeping that house on?"

"I am. I don't know quite how yet but it's my home and I'm staying on in it."

"Mrs. Toogood won't be with you, you know."

"I won't be able to afford her anyway. And with the baby gone there shouldn't be much to do. Well, I must get back to the shop." She rose and so did her companion. "Are you going directly home?"

"After I stop at the chemist's and have a couple of prescriptions filled."

As they left the inn Irene asked, "Would you like me to take your case? I'll bring it home with me." She exclaimed, "Why, this is Gillian's."

"Mrs. Toogood lent it so I wouldn't have to lug that big one of mine around. Do you mind?"

"Why should I? See you this evening." Irene stopped and called, "What are you doing this afternoon?"

"Having a nap," Miss Sanderson told her with great satisfaction.

That is exactly what she did. She paused and hugged Lucy and then fished in her shopping bag. Taking the pattern book and wool, she handed them to the housekeeper. "I was going to make up a sweater for Lucy but there won't be time. Can you use these?"

"Sure can, miss. What a pretty green. Be just right for my youngest. Mollie's got kinda reddish hair." She added regretfully, "But Mollie's not as pretty as little Lucy."

"No one," Miss Sanderson told the baby, "is as pretty as you."

Then she went to her room and curled up under a down comforter. *If I can't sleep at night,* she told herself drowsily, I'll do it in the daytime while the staunch Mrs. Toogood is here to ward off fiends. Anyway, two more days and that fiend would trouble her slumbers no more.

That night Forsythe was as restless as his secretary. While Miss Sanderson started up and slipped out of bed to pad barefooted into the nursery, her employer twisted in a tangle of sheets, staring at the shadowy ceiling.

About the time that Irene Markham turned the hood of her shabby little car toward London the following morning, Forsythe, in robe and slippers, was disturbing Sergeant Brummell's sleep.

"Awful early, sir," the sergeant mumbled. "Hardly daybreak."

"Any progress, Beau?"

"Not yesterday, sir. Maybe we'll have better luck today."

"I've a feeling this is important and time is of the essence."

Brummell's voice was more alert. "Think you're on to something?"

"I've this feeling . . ."

"Like Miss Sanderson's fey feeling?"

"Similar. Beau, get back to me the moment you have something. I'll be here in my flat waiting."

There was a pause and then the other man asked, "Care to give me a hint, sir?"

"Lucy Foster is leaving Maddersley tomorrow."

"Ah, I see what you're getting at. I'll do my best, Mr. Forsythe."

The barrister rang off. He felt a bit reassured. Sergeant Brummell's best was generally very good indeed.

THIRTEEN

IT WAS AFTER NINE when Miss Sanderson got out of her rumpled bed and showered. She pulled on a robe and slippers and padded down to the kitchen to find the housekeeper hovering over the stove and the baby perched on her high chair. She chucked Lucy under the chin and asked, "Miss Markham away?"

"At the crack of dawn, miss. Had me come early and left soon's I stuck my nose in the door. Making up waffles and sausage for breakfast. That all right with you?"

"Fine." Bending, Miss Sanderson picked up Lucy's stuffed lamb. "You're staying the night with us?"

"Promised Miss Irene I would. Brought a little bag with me. Miss Irene said I could sleep in one of the boys' bunk beds."

"It's awfully decent of you."

The housekeeper slid a steaming platter on the table and beamed. "Tell the truth, miss, it's gonna be a treat for me. Having six kiddies in that poky house can be a trial. Bert's taking care of them and Mrs. Rugg—she's right next door to us—promised to look in on them." She attacked her breakfast with gusto. "Figure I'll cook us a good lunch and there's lamb chops for supper. There's a couple of dandy shows on the telly tonight or we could play a game of rummy. You play rummy, miss?"

"I haven't played it in years."

"Like bicycling, never forget how. You'll do fine."

As soon as breakfast was finished Mrs. Toogood shooed Miss Sanderson out of the kitchen. Lucy held up imploring arms and Miss Sanderson scooped her up and carried her to the living room. She deposited the baby on thick salmon carpeting and rummaged in the toy box for blocks. As soon as the block house was finished the baby, with a triumphant crow, knocked it flying. Patiently Miss Sanderson built another one.

The morning passed peacefully and after a hearty lunch Miss Sanderson put Lucy down for her nap. While she was upstairs she slipped off her robe and pulled on a heavy tweed skirt and a woolen pullover. Then she returned to the living room and picked up a magazine. While she leafed through it she could hear the hum of a vacuum cleaner. The machine shut off and a tousled head craned around the door. "Any plans for this afternoon, miss? Got the work just about finished."

Wary of being inveigled into a game of rummy Miss Sanderson said, "When Lucy wakes up I'll take her out for a walk. We could both use a breath of air. Where's her pram kept?"

"On the veranda. Got a piece of canvas over it. Be sure to cover it up when you get back. Pram could get horrible damp." Wandering over, the housekeeper peered between striped curtains. "Hope the fog holds off till you get back."

Miss Sanderson joined her and looked over the heavy shoulder. "Why, it's quite clear."

"Right now. But the wind's changing and fog is coming.

Can smell it. Get a powerful lot of fog this time of year."
The phone rang and she nudged Miss Sanderson. "Bet you
that'll be Miss Irene, asking how you're making out. You
better get it."

It wasn't Irene Markham's light high voice. This voice
was male and rather gruff. She called, "Mrs. Toogood, it's
for you."

"Bert . . . when? . . . how high? Well, you get over to
the chemist's and get one. And you ring back soon's you
take them." Slamming down the receiver, the housekeeper
turned a wrathful face to her companion. "If that don't beat
all! That Bert is the clumsiest man ever born. Broke the
thermometer, he did. Now we gotta buy a new one."

"What's wrong?"

"The twins. Percy and Willy. Bert says when he got
them up they was all flushed and fretting. He waited a
while and they got worse." She snapped her fingers. "Bet I
know what it is! Let them play with Joey Rugg when he
was coming down with the chicken pox. Didn't know the
boy was ailing and that Mrs. Rugg didn't say a word.
Didn't care if my kids got sick!"

Conscious of a sinking feeling in the pit of her stomach
Miss Sanderson prowled up and down the hall waiting for
Bert Toogood to report back. It took some time. When
the phone rang she jumped. This conversation was as brief
as the first and when Mrs. Toogood rang off she looked
worried. "Temperatures of both little chaps is way over a
hundred. Percy and Willy are both pretty sick though Bert
says he thinks Willy is the worst." She was twisting her
apron in both hands. "Give Miss Irene my word I wouldn't
budge outta this house till she gets back tomorrow. Don't
want to leave you alone here. What's a body to do?"

"What you must." Miss Sanderson patted her arm. "Your place is with your children."

"Know that, miss. Not even a doctor here now. Have to take them over to Lambert. Well, better get my duds together." She headed up the stairs. When she came down she was carrying a shabby carpetbag. While Miss Sanderson helped her on with her coat Mrs. Toogood rattled off instructions at high speed. "Supper in the fridge. All you gotta do is stick them chops under the broiler. If'n you want to keep the baby down here for a time this evening get her basket outta the laundry room. Missus used that basket a lot. Mr. Johnston made it up for her." She buttoned the coat and pulled her woolen hat down over her ears. "Bottles for Lucy all made up. Give her some of that minced beef and peas for supper. If'n you get nervous ring up Mr. Johnston. He's a nice old fellow and tell you straight I never did agree with Miss Irene keeping him outta this house after the missus passed on."

Tucking her plastic purse under an arm, she bent for her bag. Miss Sanderson unchained the door and held it open. The housekeeper's prediction was coming true. Threads of mist spiraled along the walk. At the edge of the veranda the housekeeper paused. "If'n you take little Lucy out for an airing don't go far. Fog's gonna get thick. And Miss Sanders . . ."

"Yes?"

"When you get back you get that chain on the door. Other two are locked but you check them anyway. Stay right in the house and don't let no one in."

"I won't."

Miss Sanderson watched the muffled figure waddling down the walk to the gate. She watched until Mrs.

Toogood was out of sight. How, she asked herself, could she ever have felt distaste for that woman? Right now she'd give anything to have the woman with her. Frowsy hair and missing tooth and all. The housekeeper had given sound advice. Perhaps she'd better skip the walk. Then she turned and looked down the shadowy hall. No, she must get out of this house for a time.

Silence pressed down and then, from the nursery, came the tentative wail of the baby. Miss Sanderson took the steps two at a time.

It took all Miss Sanderson's strength to get the high-wheeled pram down the flight of steep steps. When she returned to the house for Lucy she was breathless. Before she shut the door she shifted the baby from one arm to the other while she checked her pockets for the key Irene had left for her. Her fingers touched metal and she closed the door and then tried it.

Tucking the baby under a blanket, she told her, "In that outfit you could take first prize at a baby show."

The comment was justified. A white fur bonnet framed the vivid little face, and hands waved matching mittens. A fur trimmed coat and leggings completed the picture. Lucy bounced and cooed and Miss Sanderson steered the unwieldy pram down the walk. Ground mist swirled around the wheels and her feet. As she passed the row of cottages she noticed mist was creeping over the shrubs in the yards. Among dark pines the vicarage was almost obscured. They reached the church and in the graveyard behind it fog swirled around grave markers pointing pallid fingers toward a pewter-colored sky. Miss Sanderson wondered which of those marble fingers stood guard over the graves of Lucy's family.

At the corner she stood indecisively and then turned the pram down toward Abercrombie's pasture. She'd have liked to have walked over the stone bridge toward Maddersley Hall but she wasn't going to jolt the baby on the gravel road. At the base of the hill the fog was thicker. In the chemist's window ruby and emerald globes glowed with eerie light. Across the street yellow lights could be discerned in all the shops but one. Irene's shop was dark.

The door of the inn opened and someone came out. Miss Sanderson couldn't tell who it was or even if it was a man or a woman. For a moment light poured across the walk and she wistfully regarded it. In a bit people would be playing darts or watching the television, people would be drinking pints and clouding the air with cigarette smoke. Paddy would be leaning across the bar and Kate poking her dark head around her kitchen door. She longed to join them but she could hardly take Lucy into a bar.

"Better get back," she told the baby and her own voice sounded hollow and remote.

Hidden in the fog she no longer had to play the part of invalid. She sped up the hill and the baby waved a fur mitten and crowed with pleasure. When they reached the crossing she found she couldn't see more than a few feet in either direction. Stopping, she strained her ears. No sound of a car. She rushed across the lane and jolted the pram roughly up on the curb. The baby gave a protesting wail. "Hush, Lucy, consider yourself fortunate. It's easier to ride than pilot this monster."

The church, graveyard, and vicarage had disappeared behind a wall of yellowish fog. So had the cottages. Miss Sanderson's loping stride covered ground rapidly but she had to slow down to locate the gate of the Markham house. As she did she heard the thud of running footsteps behind her. She spun around and a figure in a white leather coat with long hair streaming from under a black tam lunged out of the fog.

"Abigail." Linda Beauchamp panted. "I've been trying to catch you all the way up the hill." She waved a brown bag. "Stopped in at the butcher shop to pick up a meat pie and I thought I saw you farther up the hill. My, but you can move *fast*."

"I was rushing to get Lucy home. This dampness may not be good for her."

The younger woman bent over the pram. "She's sweet!"

"I thought you didn't like children?"

"I don't mind babies. They're so *harmless*. Too bad they have to grow up." Bulging brown eyes brushed over Miss Sanderson's face. "I heard about the Toogood twins—how sick they are. And I thought of *you*, all alone in that dreadful house."

"In Maddersley news travels with the speed of light."

"Doesn't it though? Kate Rourke was in the chemist's when Bert Toogood came in to buy a thermometer. He told Kate his wife was going to have to go home and look after the twins. And everyone knows Irene Markham drove to London this morning."

"I'd hate to try to keep a secret in this place."

"Oh, there are *secrets*," the young woman said darkly. "I've been thinking how I can help. You were so *decent* to me the other day. I couldn't bear to spend the night in that house but perhaps you would like to bring the baby to my cottage. I've only a camp bed but I could sleep on the floor and you can have the cot."

"I wouldn't dream of putting you out of your bed."

"And that was a silly idea, Miss Beauchamp," a voice snapped in Miss Sanderson's ear. Whirling, she faced a tall bulky figure draped in a dark cape with a hood pulled low over the face. Under the hood wire-rimmed glasses glinted. "Sleep on a cold floor and you'll be a sick girl. Miss Sanders and the baby will be better off in the Markham house. I must admit it is comfortable and warm."

"Nurse Ines, the villagers say that house is *cursed*," Linda wailed.

"Balderdash, Miss Beauchamp! You're an educated woman. Surely you don't believe that sort of rubbish."

"They say many people have died violently in it." The girl lowered her voice to a whisper. "They say blood calls for *blood*."

"And I say the villagers are still back in the dark ages. If they could find a witch they would burn her. Now you get right along home, my girl, and make up a pot of strong tea. That'll settle you down."

It was an order and the girl didn't argue. She turned away and fog swallowed her up. Nurse Ines chuckled. "Bundle of nerves. No business living alone. Miss Sanders, you get that baby right in the house. You're right, she shouldn't be out in this damp. Need help getting the pram up?"

"No," Miss Sanderson said firmly.

She fumbled at the gate and the nurse stepped forward and opened it. As she humped the pram up the steps she wondered how long the woman had been standing silently in the fog. Long enough to have heard her remark about damp.

She unlocked the door, lifted the baby from the nest of blankets, and threw the canvas cover over the pram. Stepping into the hall, she clicked a switch. Light streamed down on black-and-white tile. She was conscious her heart was thudding. Could those women have frightened her?

She used Nurse Ines' word. Balderdash. But one thing was definite. By this time the entire population of the village knew she was alone. That thought was far from comforting.

She put the baby down in the lounge and took off her coat. By the time it was hung in the hall closet Lucy had managed to crawl over to a table and pull herself up, and she was now reaching for a vase.

"You are an imp," Miss Sanderson scolded. "And the way it looks you're soon going to be a walking imp."

She took off the baby's bonnet and coat and was working at the leggings when the telephone rang. "Better come with me, imp," she said and hoisted Lucy from the floor. Holding the baby balanced on one hip, she lifted the receiver. The voice was fruity and rich and was one she recognized immediately. "It has been brought to my attention," the vicar said, "that you've been . . . hem . . . deserted by Mrs. Toogood."

"Two of her children are ill."

"Yes, the twins. Chicken pox, I believe. It occurred to me that with the fog you may be somewhat uneasy. Mrs. Gay could make up a room for you and the child. We do have many unoccupied rooms but I must warn you they're unaired and may be quite damp."

Miss Sanderson had a flash of Lucy and her crouching in a clammy room in that cold dark house. She would take her chances here. Cursed or not the beds weren't damp. "Very kind of you, Dr. Clay, but we'll be fine here."

"I hope so, dear lady." He didn't sound overly optimistic. "Should you change your mind you need only ring me up."

"Fat chance of that," she told the wriggling baby. She pulled off the leggings and felt the round bottom. "Now you're *damp*. Blimey, how many nappies do you go through in a day?"

Her foot was on the bottom step of the staircase when the phone pealed again. Still clasping the wet bottom she retraced her steps. This voice she recognized too. The decisive tones of Nurse Ines.

"After I left you I had second thoughts," the nurse announced. "Do you have the wind up over there?"

"Why do you ask?"

"The villagers have probably been filling your ears with dire tales. And then Miss Beauchamp and her wild imagination. I wondered . . ."

"As you said it's balderdash."

"Of course. But you're welcome to stay with me. I'm in the middle of packing, of course, and everything's frightfully muddled. I've only one bed so we'd have to share. Lucy could sleep in her pram."

Miss Sanderson shuddered at the thought of sharing a bed with Nurse Ines. After all, this woman was a prime candidate for mass murderer. She politely declined the offer and rang off.

She shifted the baby. "You're not only damp but you weigh a ton."

Another sound blasted the silence. This time it was the William Tell Overture. Exasperated, she was about to tear off the chain when she, like Nurse Ines, had second thoughts. Leaving the chain in place, she inched the door open a crack and applied one eye to it. All she could see was a form looming out of the fog. A dark object was thrust at her and she jumped back. "Your meat order," the dark form said.

She discerned Rog Austin holding out a small carton. "I didn't put in an order."

"Maybe Miss Markham did."

"If she had she would have told me."

He moved and light from the hall fell over his face, colorless eyes and moist girlish mouth and fall-away chin. "All right if I come in and ring up my dad? Musta got the wrong name on this here box."

Her hand was reaching for the chain. It stopped abruptly. She wasn't letting Rog Austin or anyone else into this house. "No," she said.

Avid eyes wandered over the portion of her face he could see. "Scairt, aren't you?" There was a note of relish in his voice. "Can't say I blame you, not after what's happened in there. But you could turn on some light. Maybe I can figure it out."

No harm in that. She switched on the veranda light. The baby had had enough and was wailing. "Hurry up," she ordered.

He lifted the carton and peered at it. "Blast dad's scrawl! Got Matthew down here. Could have sworn it was Markham. This is for next door. Sorry to bother you."

She banged the door shut. I'll leave the veranda light on, she decided. This time she not only got upstairs but managed to change Lucy's nappies and slip her into coveralls. The baby was still fretting. Hungry, Miss Sanderson thought, which makes two of us. "An army," she said aloud, "marches on its stomachs. We'll fill ours."

Lucy had the priority. She ate the noxious-looking mince and peas in her usual carefree manner. Part of it went on her tray, part smudged her face and hands, some of it went on Miss Sanderson when she smiled charmingly and blew a mouthful directly into her nursemaid's face.

Miss Sanderson mopped at her face. "I've an inspired idea how to feed you, imp. Both of us strip and get in the bathtub. When you've finished chucking your meal around I turn on the shower. Think I'll write a how-to book on babies. Put your picture on the cover and it should be a best-seller." The baby gurgled and she added, "And you're a great conversationalist. How about some applesauce?"

After the baby was fed, washed, and put in the playpen with a bottle clutched in her plump hands, Miss Sanderson opened the fridge door. Ah, dinner was indeed ready. Mrs. Toogood had made a salad, laid out six plump lamb chops, a plate of cheese rolls, and a jar of mint sauce. There was also apple tart. Too bad the housekeeper was missing this bounteous repast. Miss Sanderson took out the salad, one roll, and hesitated over the chops. Finally she decided on two. When the broiler had been switched on she lighted a cigarette and waited for the stove to come up to heat.

The telephone sent a strident summons and she swore and trotted down the hall. "Mary Maddersley," a crisp voice told her. "I understand you were in London yesterday. Did you see your physician?"

"No."

"I thought not. I felt you had gone to . . . to report." The line hummed and then she said, "Did you lie to me about not being connected with the police?"

Time to put some cards on the table, Miss Sanderson decided. "I'm not a member of the police force, Miss Maddersley, but in the past I have been involved with police officers. I'm also no relation to the Markhams."

"I didn't think you were." There was another pause and when Miss Maddersley spoke her voice wasn't as crisp. "Now the police will be back. Miss Sanders, or whoever you really are, my brother can't stand up under an interrogation. Do you know Chief Inspector Kepesake?"

"Yes. He's competent and fair. I hardly think he'll be brutal with your brother."

"Perhaps I misjudged the man. I want you to know I hold nothing against you. I'm aware you're doing what is necessary. And I haven't breathed a word about you to anyone else."

"Not even to your brother?"

"Particularly not to Donnie." The voice again became crisp. "One thing I shan't worry about. You'll be fine in that house. I should imagine you know how to handle yourself."

As Miss Sanderson returned to the kitchen she made a wry grimace. Miss Maddersley probably imagined she held the black belt in jujitsu or excelled in a similar form of martial art. Robby had been accurate when he'd told Adam Kepesake she had absolutely no training. Even if she did have a revolver she wouldn't know how to use it.

Pausing by the playpen, she smiled down at Lucy. The milk in the bottle was fast disappearing. She pulled the curtains over the big window and closed the shorter ones on the glassed section set in the back door. She noticed fog had crept right up against the panes.

When the chops were broiled they looked delectable but she found her appetite had vanished. She ate part of one and nibbled at a roll. Pushing the plate away, she considered having a large drink of the whiskey purchased by Mrs. Sutter. Better not. "This house," she informed the baby, "is enough to drive one to drink."

As she was stacking the dishes in the dishwashing machine the door chimes pealed lustily. She moved slowly down the hall. Despite lights blazing in the hall and the lounge, shadows seemed to crouch in doorways and huddle under the staircase. As she passed the darkened dining room she paused to flip on the chandelier. This time she made no move to detach the chain. She inched the door open and peered out. The overhead light on the veranda illuminated a tall figure dressed in loose oilskins and high rubber boots. Both hands were thrust in slash pockets. He stood well back, near the steps. She'd never seen him before.

"Miss Sanders?" he said hesitantly. "We haven't met. I'm Donald Maddersley."

"I have met your sister."

"Mary sent me around. She . . . we both feel it a poor idea for you to be here alone. We thought you might consider coming to the Hall for the night."

"Your sister rang up a short time ago." Her nails were biting painfully into the palms of her hands. "She didn't mention anything about this."

He moved a step closer. His hands were still jammed in his pockets. Was there anything else in those pockets, she wondered. They were deep enough to hold a long sharp knife. "This house, Miss Sanders, has a bad history. Horrible things have happened here. A woman and child are not safe in it. I urge you to bring the baby and come with me. Open the door and I'll wait while you get ready."

"No!"

"Don't be frightened. I'll admit this wasn't Mary's idea but—"

"Go *away!*"

She banged the door shut and jumped back. Her heart was racing and she was breathing heavily. Then she moved the few feet and pressed an ear against the panel. Was he moving across the veranda, down the steps? She could hear nothing. Was he circling the house, looking for a way in? God! She hadn't checked the surgery door. She wrenched open the door to the waiting room, turned on the switch, ran over to the exterior door. It was locked.

She glanced around. Light from the waiting room spilled through the doorway to the office. The office where Paul Foster's mutilated body had slumped back in his chair, where blood had spattered the walls and . . .

She fled from the surgery, down the hall, pushing the swinging door open. Running across the tile floor, she yanked at the door handle. Locked. She slumped down at the table and buried her face in her hands. Nothing here but the tick of the wall clock, the soft purr of Lucy's breathing, the comforting odor of broiled lamb.

She glanced up at the clock. Only a little past six. Hours until this night was over and daylight and Irene Markham and Leonard Foster arrived. Long dark hours in this fog-shrouded house. From outside . . . with knives. Was Maddersley still out there? Was Nurse Ines in her long dark cape or Paddy Rourke, his Irish eyes no longer merry, moving stealthily through the fog? Had Irene Markham's trip to London been feigned? Was she even now circling back to the village to destroy the last member of her sister's family?

With no compunction Miss Sanderson opened a cupboard and took down the squat brown bottle. Pouring out a couple of inches, she downed it like a dose of medicine.

"There comes a time," she told the baby shakily, "for demon drink. There comes a time for all good cowards to come to the aid of their sanity. It's my Scottish grandmother who's to blame for my present state. Granny MacPherson was a firm believer in ghosties and curses and things that go bong in the night. She carried a rabbit's foot and possibly strung garlic around her neck. But tomorrow your aunt and uncle will be here and they'll take you to a nice safe home where you'll have cousins to grow up with. I must be very pleasant to them and perhaps they'll extend visiting privileges to me. I'll go to see you at Christmas and take a present. Maybe a big doll with ringlets like yours . . . And if you think I'm talking too much you're right. I'm babbling away like Linda Beauchamp and for the same reason. I'm nervous. What the hell! I'm terrified. Shaking in my boots."

The baby didn't even gurgle. The bottle had fallen from her hand and coppery lashes were drifting down against her cheeks. Her chin was decorated with a drop of milk. And I'm not taking you up to the nursery, Miss Sanderson told the child silently. I want you right where I can see you. That basket Mrs. Toogood had mentioned . . . I'll tuck you up, take you to the living room, light a fire to ward off evil, and there we'll spend the night.

She found the basket in a corner of the laundry room. It was fashioned ingeniously of a wicker basket suspended on a metal stand. It had small wheels and a leather strap with which to rock the basket. The mattress was covered with a sheet patterned with ducks, and a matching blanket was folded across the bottom. Lucy didn't rouse when she was lifted into the basket and the blanket was drawn over her. She slept soundly as the basket trundled along black-and-white tile into the living room. Mrs. Toogood had laid the fire and in moments paper and kindling were blazing. Sitting back on her heels, Miss Sanderson positioned a log. Her head jerked up. A noise. But where?

She was on her feet, standing over the basket, her knuckles whitening as she grasped the poker. Another sound—at the back of the house. She looked down at the baby and then moved slowly to the hall. Her breath catching in her throat, she forced herself to the kitchen door and swung it open. Someone was knocking at the door. Clutching the poker, she crossed the floor and stood at the door. She eased a curtain to one side and looked out. She could see nothing but fog. She reached for the switch and turned on the porch light. Still nothing. Then there was movement. A hand was flung up, a big capable hand with a calloused palm—a carpenter's hand. Standing on tiptoes, she pressed her nose against the glass and peered down. A tweed cap and a wide furrowed face. With no hesitation she threw the door open.

"Matthew! Thank God!"

FOURTEEN

MATTHEW JOHNSTON LOOKED FROM the poker in her hand to her ashen face. "Spooked, eh? Thought you might be. That's why I came over. To remind you I'm right next door and if anything bothers you you've only to ring up and I'll be right over."

Lowering the poker, she stepped aside. "Come in."

The tweed cap moved from side to side. "Can't, Abigail. Don't go any place I'm not welcome. And Irene made it plain I'm not welcome in her house."

He started to turn the chair toward the ramp and she reached out and grabbed an arm of it. *"Please.* For God's sake, Matthew, I'm nearly out of my mind."

"If Irene hears about it you'll be in for it."

"Irene can go straight to hell!"

He chuckled. "Nothing wrong with your spirit. All right, get out of the way so's I can get this chair in."

He wheeled in and she retreated to a chair. Her knees felt as though they'd turned to jelly. Johnston flipped his cap onto one of the pegs with a single dextrous movement and straightened the folds of his rug. "What got you in this state, Abigail?"

"People." She realized she was still clinging to the poker. She propped it up against the chair leg. "People coming to the door, ringing up."

"Tell me about it."

She told him. He listened and then said, "Villagers may be nosy and gossipy and kind of standoffish but they're good people. Maybe you should have gone to the vicarage or to Nurse Ines or—"

"How could I? Someone in this village killed Lucy's family."

He rubbed his chin. "Tell you what. I could stay the night. Sit in the living room. Don't sleep much anyway so it wouldn't be a hardship." He looked around. "Where's the wee one? Tucked up in bed?"

"Lucy's in the living room. I couldn't bear her out of my sight. She's sound asleep in that basket you made for her."

"Well, must admit that's as comfortable as anything can be. Took a lot of pains making it."

Reaching for the bottle, she spilled scotch in her glass. "Would you like a drink, Matthew?"

"Don't touch spirits. Only have a pint now and then. And you leave that stuff alone. Strong tea's better for you. I'll brew a pot."

She smiled. "You sound exactly like Nurse Ines."

"Nice woman. Some people don't care for her but she's been kind to me. Since Paul died she's been dropping in every day to see how I'm making out. Even massages my legs for me. Hurt something fierce at times. Now, I'll make that tea. No, sit where you are. Not sensible for you with that heart condition to get so upset. And I know my way around this kitchen as well as I do my own." He took a canister off the counter and reached for the kettle. "Doctor have some news for you yesterday?"

"The results of all of the tests aren't in yet." Miss Sanderson found she was relaxing. She watched him fill the kettle, take down a tray, reach under the counter for cups.

"Won't bother with milk or sugar. Noticed the other day you take yours clear too." He rinsed out the teapot with hot water, measured in tea leaves, and poured boiling water. "You know, Abigail, people with good health don't know how lucky they are. Like me before the accident. No money can buy back health. But I guess you know that."

Miss Sanderson was tempted to tell him the truth, that her health was excellent. She changed her mind. Matthew might consider she'd lied to him, which she had, and desert her. And I need you, she told the man silently, I really need you. Instead she said, "Shall we have our tea in the living room? I would like to be near Lucy."

"You go along and I'll bring the tray." His eyes twinkled. "And use that poker for what it's meant for, stirring up the fire."

She'd forgotten both the poker and the fire. She carried it with her and built up the fire. In moments she heard the wheels of his chair rumbling over the floor of the hall. He steered the chair in on the other side of the basket and deposited the tray on a low table. "Shall I be mother?"

She nodded and he picked up the pot. Then his head jerked up. "What is it, Matthew?"

"Thought I heard something." He shrugged. "Must be a board creaking. Houses are full of noises."

"Don't I know *that*." She turned her head toward the hall, listening. The telephone pealed and she jumped. "Damn! Another well-wisher."

"If it's Irene better not tell her I'm in her precious house."

"You can count on me."

It wasn't Irene. It was Robby's voice. "Sandy. Are you alone?"

"No."

"In that case mention Dr. Forbes."

"You're ringing up rather late, Dr. Forbes."

"Now listen. Brummell says Miss Markham is in London."

"Yes, doctor."

His voice was edged with strain. "Don't mention who's with you. We have the name of the murderer. Sandy, for God's sake say something!"

"You have the results of the tests," she babbled. "Can you give them to me?"

He told her the name of the murderer. She reached out to the telephone stand and clutched at it for support. "Sandy," he whispered.

"I think," she said clearly, "I agree with you. The situation does seem extremely serious."

"Hold on! We'll be there!"

With a shaking hand, as though handling something fragile, she kept the receiver in place and spoke to a humming line. "It was good of you to let me know . . . No, I won't panic . . . Yes, I'll go to your office as soon as I get to London tomorrow. Goodnight, Dr. Forbes."

Still clinging to the telephone stand, she thought, it's all right that I'm trembling, that is only natural. Now . . .

Matthew Johnston had already poured the tea and steam spiraled up from the cups. The fire was crackling cheerily and in the basket Lucy peacefully slept. Miss Sanderson stood behind her chair, her hands reaching for its back for support. It all looked so . . . so *cosy.*

Matthew raised his head and youthful eyes in his

wrinkled face met her own. "Couldn't help overhearing. Bad news, Abigail?"

"Disturbing. The results of the tests."

"Your heart?" She nodded and he said reassuringly, "Don't go thinking the worst. Tests can be wrong. Should know. Spent a lot of time in hospitals. Dr. Brown used to joke that I was there more than he was."

She lifted her head. "Matthew! Now *I* hear something. At the back of the house. Can you remember whether I shut that door properly after you came in?"

"Didn't notice. Where are you going?"

"I'd better have a look."

"No." He swung his chair around. "You sit down. I'll have a look."

It didn't take long. The chair wheeled back and he pulled it up by the basket. "Door's locked. Spooking yourself again. Glad to see you're drinking your tea. That'll settle your nerves." He lifted his cup and took a gulp. "Little bitter. Too strong do you think?"

"Just right."

"Want me to stay down here while you and Lucy sleep?"

She drained her cup. "I would appreciate it. You say you don't sleep soundly?"

"Hardly sleep at all. Haven't since the accident. Pain seems worse at night. Told Paul about it and he really had at me. Said I should have mentioned it before. I told him the truth. Hate drugs and never've been able to swallow pills or capsules properly. Paul said he could fix that. Took a bottle of liquid out of his cupboard and poured out some in a smaller bottle. I told him I didn't like to think what folks would say if they heard I was taking that stuff, and he winked and said even Nurse Ines would never know. Said it would be our little secret."

Miss Sanderson extended her cup and he tilted the teapot over it. She noticed her hand was now steady. She thought, with dreadful clarity I see the fiend that close behind me has been treading. Her voice was as steady as her hand. "Did the drug help you sleep?"

"Wouldn't know. Never used it. Saved it. Came in handy too." His hand, holding a knife, came out from under the tartan rug. An ordinary butcher knife with a long thin blade, she thought dully. "Sit steady, Abigail. Moved that poker where you can't reach it. Know you have use of your legs but you can't move that fast. Been watching you. Don't try to run for it or—" He shifted the knife and poised it over the sleeping baby. "You move and she's dead."

"Don't."

He put the knife back in his lap. "Just remember there's nothing wrong with my arms. Fact is, my shoulders and arms are stronger than most folks'—from wheeling this chair and swinging myself in and out of it." He picked up his cup and emptied it.

"Why?" she whispered.

"Sit back and listen. You won't be upset much longer. Put the rest of that drug in your tea. Wasn't much left and may not work too fast but in a while you'll be getting drowsy." With his left hand he emptied the teapot into his cup. "All my life I've prided myself on being an honest man. Ask anyone in Cheltenham. Matthew Johnston, they'll tell you, is honest and never tells a lie. But I've been lying a lot this last year. The day we met, Abigail, I told you lies.

"Lied about my daughter's death. Ariel didn't die from a ruptured appendix. She died because some man had gotten her pregnant and she'd been aborted. Bungled job and by the time Ariel got home to Julia and me she was hemorrhaging. I was all for taking our girl to the hospital but Julia wouldn't hear of it. 'Matthew,' Julia says, 'I can't bear to have our daughter's name besmirched. Get Dr. Brown. He'll save Ariel.' I got him but he couldn't save her. Ariel died in my arms." His fingers closed around the handle of the knife. "Begged my girl to tell me who did it. All she would say was her lover had done the abortion. Then, at the end, she whispered a name. Paul!"

"Paul."

"That's all she said." He turned his head and firelight glinted ruddily across his face. "Julia never got over Ariel's death. Something broke inside her. She killed herself in that car and nearly killed me. Julia drove off the road into a gully and it was nearly two hours before someone noticed and they came for us. I was trapped, couldn't move, and I lay there, looking into her dead face. How I *loved* her. Swore I would find the man who'd killed her and our daughter. Took years to track him down. I was in and out of hospitals, operation after operation. Pain all the time. Pain in my legs and my heart. Then I got his name."

"How?"

"After we buried our daughter I went to London to try and find Paul. Ariel didn't have any close friends but I questioned the students at her ballet school. One of the girls told me she'd seen a man pick Ariel up several times from school. Said he was young and dark and nice looking. But she didn't know his name. Then I went to the house where Ariel had boarded. Her landlady was real fond of my girl but she didn't know anything about Paul.

"The landlady took me up to Ariel's room and helped me pack her clothes and things. I thought there might be let-

ters or a diary to show me the way but there wasn't anything. Seemed queer because Ariel, from the time she was
about eight, always kept a diary."

"There were no leads to Paul?"

"None. After Julia died I kept wondering how to find
him. Thought of him walking around on two legs while I
was a cripple. Thought of him taking my lovely daughter
to some run-down hotel and butchering her in a filthy
room. He killed not only my daughter but my unborn
grandchild. He killed Julia. He took my family away from
me. He took my *legs*. Promised myself and God I would
find him and take everything away from him."

Miss Sanderson sagged in her chair, resolutely keeping
her eyes away from Lucy's sleeping face. How long will it
take Robby, she wondered. Fog will slow him. Oh God,
Robby, hurry! Johnston's big head tilted toward the baby.
Must keep him talking. "How did you find Paul Foster?"

Hectically brilliant eyes jerked back to her. "Fourteen
months ago my prayers were answered. Got a package in
the post from Ariel's landlady. She'd been having renova-
tions done on her house and when the carpenter pulled out
the wardrobe in the girl's room he found Ariel's diary. It'd
slipped down between warped boards. From her grave my
little girl was pointing the way for her daddy.

"Ariel wrote about meeting this medical student and she
raved on about how they loved each other. Said how
she went to her Paul when she found she was with child.
She figured he would marry her but he told her he
couldn't. He was starting his career and he couldn't afford
a family. Paul talked Ariel into letting him abort the baby.
She gave his last name and where he'd gone to school and
the hospital he was at and—"

"But Paul Foster was a *good* doctor. How could he have bungled the abortion?"

"No practical experience then. Didn't know what he was doing but did it anyway." Johnston smiled happily. "From then on it was easy. I wrote right off to the medical association and got this address. Then I sold our home and went to an estate agent. Found two rental houses here— the cottage Linda Beauchamp has and the one next door to here. Took that. God was helping me. So I came to Maddersley to kill Paul Foster."

She rubbed at her brow. "And now you'll kill Lucy and me."

"Last chance I'll get. She's leaving tomorrow. And I'll have to kill you too, Abigail. Don't want to but can't help it. With that heart condition you wouldn't last much longer anyway. You won't feel a thing. Be asleep and I'll slide this knife in like I did with Gillian and Arthur and Andrew."

He glanced down at Lucy again and Miss Sanderson said quickly, "Why did you wait so long? You were here over a year."

"Gillian. I wasn't lying when I told you how much I liked her. She was sweet and kind to me and I knew to get at Paul what I would have to do to her and couldn't bring myself to do it. But then something happened—"

"Melanie Marlow."

"You're a bright lady, Abigail. Yes, Melanie. Must admit I didn't take to the girl. She was a saucy little baggage but she was young and her dad would have handled her same as he did her mother. But Gillian hired the girl as a maid and took her into this house and then when she found Paul was interested in Melanie she got rid of her. Didn't bother

sending Melanie back to her folks. Oh no, Gillian gave
Melanie some money and didn't care where the child went
or what happened to her."

"That woman," Miss Sanderson said. "*That terrible, terrible
woman.* You weren't talking about Nell Austin."

"I was talking about Gillian Foster." His eyes blazed.
"The scales fell from my eyes and I saw Gillian as she really
was. Ernie Marlow may have been shouting but it was a
cry from a father's heart. And Gillian *laughed* at him and
threatened to have her fine doctor husband tell the police
Ernie had abused his daughter. After she threw Ernie and
the Austins out she came back to the kitchen and bragged
to Mrs. Toogood and me."

"So you poisoned the dogs."

"Hated to do that but to get to Gillian I had to get rid of
Wolf. He would have torn me to ribbons. Used some rat
poison I found in my gardening shed and made up balls of
mince and threw them to Wolf and Dora Campbell's dog
and Paddy's terrier."

He ran a lingering finger along the knife blade. Talk,
Miss Sanderson thought, keep him talking. "Had you made
plans to kill the Foster family on the eve of the birthday
party?"

"Knew it had to be soon. They were leaving and it
would have been hard to get at them in London. But the
afternoon I helped Gillian with the party stuff she said
Irene was coming along right after work to help out. Mrs.
Toogood and Nurse Ines would be here until Irene arrived.
So I figured I wouldn't be able to do it that evening. Then,
just as I was getting ready to go home, Irene phoned.
Gillian said, 'You have to work late tonight? Oh, that's all
right. Matthew's been helping me and all I have to do now
is some baking. Oh, you'll bring the cake after nine.'"

He smiled and Miss Sanderson shuddered. Mad, completely mad. Driven mad by grief and revenge and unrelenting pain. He stretched thick arms and the hand holding the knife lingered over the basket. "I did tell you the truth about what I did when I went home. I wrapped Arthur's model kit up real nice and then I went and sat by the window in the sitting room. I saw Nurse Ines come out of here and go into her cottage. Saw Mrs. Toogood on her way home. Knew it was then or never.

"When I knocked at the kitchen door Gillian was sure surprised to see me back. I showed her the present and said I wanted to put it in the laundry room with the rest of the birthday stuff. She was getting vegetables out of the fridge and she said to go right ahead. When I wheeled back into the kitchen she was sitting at the table. I told her she looked awful tired and did she want me to brew tea for her and Paul. Gillian was all for that and told me to give the boys a drink of orange juice."

He looked at Miss Sanderson as though waiting to be complimented. Her head lolled back against the chair and she watched him through slitted eyes. "Won't be long now, Abigail. Soon you'll be asleep and . . ." He stretched his giant torso. "Haven't felt so peaceful and relaxed for years. My work's just about finished. Feels good to tell someone about it. And there's no danger of you talking. Where was I?"

"Putting the drug in the cups and glasses."

"Took them in to Paul and the boys and then went back to the kitchen and waited. Didn't take long. Gillian's head fell forward and I just folded her forward and—" The knife rose and slashed down in a gleaming arc. "Did the same with the boys. Fast and painless. When I got to Paul's office I kind of went wild. Ripped him right open. Had sense enough to get my chair back fast when the blood started to spout out of him. But I got blood all over my hands and some spatters on my rug. For a time I sat there and watched him. Thought about Ariel and Julia. Then I went into the waiting room and opened the door a crack and smeared his blood all over the woodwork around it so—"

"Why didn't you leave fingerprints?"

"Forgot to mention before I started that I got a pair of Paul's surgical gloves out of the supply cupboard. When I finished I pulled them off inside out and stuck them right in here." He patted the leather satchel dangling from the arm of his chair. "Pretty smart, eh? Knew the police would figure the killer left through that door and no way a cripple in a wheelchair could have gotten down those steps. All I had to do then was fix things up nice and peaceful, pick up my present, and get along home."

"You took time to position the bodies, build up the fire, switch the television program. Why?"

Rage flared redly in the youthful eyes. "Paul and Gillian prided themselves on their grand home. I wanted to remember all of them sitting in it, surrounded by those comforts they could no longer enjoy. I wanted to remember what I'd taken away from my daughter's butcher."

Robby, she thought, hurry! I can't hold him much longer. She mumbled, "How did you conceal the cause of your daughter's death?"

"Easy. I told you Dr. Brown was Ariel's godfather. Julia begged him not to put down the cause of our daughter's death on the certificate. So he didn't. The only ones who knew how Ariel really died were Julia and I and Dr. Brown."

"How could you bear to kill Andrew and Arthur?"

"Didn't bother me a bit. Lied to you about liking those

boys. They were mean little demons. When we were alone those boys called me Uncle Gimpy, and Arthur kicked me right here"—he rubbed a twisted leg—"when I wouldn't buy him an ice cream. Killing those dogs bothered me more." He drew his wrist across his eyes. "I'm going to sleep tonight. From now on I'm going to sleep better than I have in years."

"Lucy has never hurt you," Miss Sanderson pleaded. "She's never hurt anyone. Matthew, for the love of God, spare her! Her aunt and uncle will raise her. She won't be like her parents or her brothers."

"Wasting your time, Abigail. Wouldn't make sense to leave her alive. Promised my dead family and God I would take the lives of Paul and *all* his family." He glared down at Lucy's rosy face. The child stirred and flung an arm over her head. "She looks just like Gillian. Got Paul Foster and Gillian in her. Grow up like them, hurting people just for the fun of it." He looked across the basket at Miss Sanderson. Her chin was resting on her chest. "Taking hold now. Soon . . ."

With a visible effort she lifted her chin. "Can I have a last drink and a cigarette?"

"No drink." He chuckled. "You would have to get up to go for the bottle. Where are your cigarettes?"

"In my handbag. Down here beside my chair."

He placed the knife blade across Lucy's throat. "Hand that bag over careful like."

She lifted the bag and held it out. Taking it with his free hand, he rummaged through the contents. "Matthew, I don't carry a weapon."

"Didn't figure you did. Pays to be careful though. Like a few more years so's I can remember the Fosters. Here, have your cigarette."

With exaggerated care she took back the handbag. Her lighter flickered and the cigarette was lit. Slowly, she put the bag on the floor and reached for a glass ashtray. Setting it on her lap, she slumped back, gray smoke wreathing around her face.

"Instead of smoking that thing you should be making a last prayer, Abigail."

"You've killed four people and are going to kill an innocent baby and you tell *me* to pray."

"I'm a God-fearing man," he told her earnestly. "Already told you God answered my prayers and led me here. Wouldn't hurt for you to ask mercy from Him."

Both his big hands and the knife were resting against the tartan rug on his lap. She ground the cigarette out in the ashtray. "Matthew," she said firmly. "God helps them who help themselves."

With all her strength she threw the heavy ashtray directly into his face. She came out of the chair with a lunge, grabbed the baby, and ran like a deer. She didn't head toward a door. She ran directly to the staircase. She bounded up the steps and stopped breathless on the top step. The baby was shrieking with outrage. Those howls were the sweetest sounds Miss Sanderson had ever heard.

She watched the wheelchair swiftly rumble to the foot of the stairs. Johnston peered up at her. A welt was raising across his brow. He rubbed at it. "You tricked me!"

She clutched the warm little body to her breast. "I tricked you about a number of things. I'm not ill and I'm not Gillian's cousin. I came to this village to find *you*. And the reason you're feeling so peaceful is because I switched the cups when I decoyed you out of the room."

"How—" He smashed his fist against the chair arm. "That phone call!"

"Right. I was given the name of the murderer who at that moment was waiting for me with drugged tea and a knife. As you said, your tea tasted bitter."

"But the Fosters went under so fast."

"You said there wasn't much drug left. You used massive doses on them." She nuzzled her chin against the baby's curls. "And now I know why Lucy wasn't killed that night. You couldn't get at her in the nursery."

"That lying Gillian! Told Mrs. Toogood she was keeping the baby downstairs and then put her to bed early." His sloping shoulders slumped. "All over now. Got to get out of here."

"Matthew, where can you go? The police will soon be here. They won't hurt you. They'll take you to someone who can help you. Wait!"

"You think I'm insane."

"You're sick. You need help. The grief for your wife and daughter . . . the constant pain . . ."

His shoulders straightened. "Matthew Johnston will never be put in an insane asylum."

Weak with exhaustion, Miss Sanderson sank down on the step. Lucy had dozed off again and she hugged the child to her. "There's no escape," she whispered.

"God will help me again. He's calling me home. Telling me to come to Julia and Ariel. Maybe . . . maybe I should have gone long since." His eyes lifted and met hers. "You've won, Abigail, and maybe I'm glad about that too. I would've hated to kill you. You never did me any harm. Pray for me."

He lifted the knife in big capable carpenter's hands and turned the blade so the tip was cutting into his chest. He threw his big torso forward. He flew out of the chair and it clattered back and hit the front door. Johnston sprawled in a tangle of tartan rug. He moaned, twisted his head, and then sighed. Blood trickled across black-and-white tile.

Miss Sanderson didn't move.

Sergeant Brummell and a uniformed constable broke the door down. The panel crashed forward, rammed the wheelchair, and sent it skittering down the hall. Chief Inspector Kepesake knelt beside Matthew Johnston's body.

With one leap Forsythe hurdled the body and ran up the steps. He gathered Miss Sanderson and the baby in his arms. His secretary pushed him away and held out the baby. She looked into his eyes. "Robby," she moaned. "This house *is* cursed. It happened again. From outside, with a knife."

Then she fainted.

FIFTEEN

DESPITE FORSYTHE'S PROTESTS MISS SANDERSON was at her desk on the following Friday morning. Although she worked with her customary speed and accuracy the other staff members eyed her warily. Young Peters, known to some as Nervous Nellie, approached the other junior.

"Can't say I think it a good idea for the old girl to be back so soon, Vincent. Have you noticed her eyes? They make shivers run up and down my spine."

Vincent, slightly older than Peters, gazed at his colleague. Under Peters' left eye a nerve jumped erratically. "If you'd been through what that old girl has," Vincent said drily, "you'd be under sedation."

Shortly after luncheon Mrs. Sutter, a brief grasped in one capable hand, entered the secretary's room. She came out faster than she'd gone in and headed straight for Forsythe's chamber.

"Wonder what's up," Peters muttered and strolled toward the coffee machine positioned to the left of Miss Sanderson's door. After a moment Vincent joined him. The clerk glanced up, rose from his desk, and sauntered over. Forsythe, with Mrs. Sutter at his heels, walked swiftly past the three men. "Back to work," he told them brusquely and shut the door in their curious faces.

Miss Sanderson sat behind her desk. A brief was spread out in front of her but she was staring directly at the barrister. Her eyes were wide and expressionless and didn't appear to see him. Her teeth were digging into her lower lip and blood trickled down her chin. From empty eyes tears traced paths down her cheeks.

"Sandy," Forsythe said tentatively. There was no response and he slapped the desk with an open hand. *"Sandy."*

"Go away. I've work to do."

Pulling a handkerchief from his pocket, he pushed it at her. "Wipe your face."

"Why? I'm perfectly all right."

He circled the desk and pulled her up. Turning her around so she faced the oval mirror, he asked harshly, "Does that look perfectly all right?"

Her eyes focused and she gazed at a white, wet, blood streaked-face. "My God!" The tears came faster. "Robby," she wailed, "what's *wrong* with me?"

He put an arm around her shoulders and eased her back in the chair. "You may have a mind like a computer but you're not a machine. You're a sensitive, compassionate woman." He took the handkerchief and dabbed at her face. "Sandy, you've been in shock and you're beginning to come out of it."

"I've felt so . . . so numb."

He slid open the bottom drawer of her desk and pulled out a bottle and two paper cups. "Brandy and this time it's medicinal."

"At least you're not pushing good strong tea." She sobbed and hiccuped and swabbed at her face.

"Down the hatch." He waited for her to drain the cup and then refilled it. Taking his own cup, he slumped in the visitor's chair. "About Maddersley—"

"*No.* I don't want to talk about it."

"Not even to hear how little Lucy is?"

"Well . . ."

"She's with her foster parents. Foster. I made a pun, Sandy. Lucy's very happy and her Uncle Leonard has decided to take a position with an oil firm in London so Lucy and his three children can have a proper home. Leonard and Marjorie Foster know what you did, how you saved the child's life. They're most grateful. They want you to come and see Lucy whenever you wish."

Miss Sanderson managed a weak, tearful smile. She shoved her cup out and he tipped the bottle over it. "Setting a bad example for the staff, Robby. I may get tiddly."

"Blast the staff and I hope you get sloshed. Right now it's the best thing in the world for you." He added carefully, "Want to hear more?"

"About what?"

"The Maddersleys. Mary Maddersley plans to rent the Hall and take her brother to Corfu for a time—"

"I thought he'd come to *kill* Lucy and me."

"No. Sir Donald was genuinely worried about you. His sister is grateful and says when they return to England you must visit them—"

"I will *never* go near that village again."

"You won't have to. The Maddersleys plan to take a smaller house with extensive grounds so Sir Donald can

continue his gardening. More good news, this time about
the Rourke family. It's come out that Paddy has secretly
been courting a buxom barmaid from Lambert and they'll
be married soon. We both have pressing invitations to a
genuine Irish wedding."

"Kate will be pleased. She'll have her grandchildren.
Any more good news?"

He grinned. "I'm not certain whether this qualifies as
good news but Beau Brummell tells me Melanie Marlow
will soon be returned to the bosom of her family. As Beau
said, it's doubtful whether even Ernie will be able to control the girl but at least he'll have a chance. The vicar has
received another church, this one in the Midlands. Reverend Clay is planning on taking his ancient housekeeper
with him.

"That man *must* be a Christian. Mrs. Gay is stone deaf
and seems utterly useless."

"Nonetheless whither the vicar goes there also goes Mrs.
Gay." Miss Sanderson's cup was again extended and he refreshed it liberally. He was pleased to see her pale blue
eyes were again alert and a tinge of color had crept into
her face. "The Toogood twins are on the mend and their
mother is going to be housekeeper for Nettie and Oscar
Seton. Irene Markham is overjoyed. Seems the genuine
Cousin Abigail is settling an annuity on Irene that will en-
able her to keep the Markham house on." Miss Sanderson
shuddered but her companion pretended not to notice.
"Miss Sanders has also given Irene the family trinkets and
the china that caused all the uproar between their respec-
tive mothers. How's that for good news?"

"How Irene can bear to stay on in that house . . .
Robby, the baby must *not* go back to that house."

"Never fear. Leonard Foster tells me little Lucy will never see the village or that house again. If Irene wants to visit her niece she'll have to come to London." Taking a deep breath, Forsythe asked, "Aren't you curious about how we got onto Johnston?"

"I don't want to talk about him."

He shrugged and dug for his pipe and leather pouch. Taking his time, he tamped tobacco, struck three matches unsuccessfully, and waited. He knew his secretary as well as she did him. An appearance of indifference always aroused her considerable curiosity. As usual it worked. She blew her nose and coughed. "If I'd had time to think about it I suppose I would have decided Dr. Brown talked."

He struck a fourth match, held it well down in the pipe bowl, and was rewarded with a mouthful of smoke. He sputtered and his eyes watered. "Eventually he did. But you were the one who gave me the killer's name."

"Me? How could I have? I didn't know myself."

"That was obvious."

"Well . . . tell me."

"Three words, Sandy. And you're the one who wrote them." She shook a baffled head and he continued, "Cast your mind back. You're meeting Matthew Johnston for the first time. You're in his kitchen and he's making tea."

Leaning her head back, she closed her eyes. "Yes?"

"He was telling you about his rug and muffler."

"Tartan. Christmas gifts from the Fosters."

"And?"

Her brow wrinkled and then her eyes snapped open. "He didn't use them until after the murders. They were pure wool and he thought them too good to use for everyday."

"Very well. Now, the day you came to London to see me you had lunch in the Fox and Crow. Mrs. Nettie Seton was there too. She came over to your table and—"

"Babbled and babbled. A detestable woman. Has a yard full of plaster gnomes."

He shook his head reproachfully. "Plaster gnomes and all Mrs. Seton managed to save your life and Lucy Foster's. Now think back. Mrs. Seton was telling you about the night of the murders. Her husband and she went to Johnston's cottage." He paused. Miss Sanderson was helping herself to brandy. "Tell me about it."

She shrugged. "She babbled on to show what a Good Samaritan she'd been. She helped the police doctor give Irene a shot to calm her and then the Setons took Irene and Lucy to their home."

"What did she say about Johnston?"

"That he couldn't help because he was holding the baby." Miss Sanderson's fine brows drew together in thought. "Lucy was crying. Mrs. Seton suggested the baby might be cold and he put a fold of—" She stopped abruptly.

"The exact words were, 'a fold of *that tartan rug.*'" Forsythe waved his pipe. "So who was lying—Nettie Seton or Matthew Johnston? Mrs. Seton had no earthly reason to lie. That left Matthew Johnston, and he must have known the Fosters were dead before Irene Markham ran over to his cottage. Incidently, Sandy, his old rug, covered with spatters of dried blood, and the surgical gloves have been found in the gardening shed behind his cottage. When I caught those words I knew I'd better check over his background again. It all seemed completely aboveboard. A fine, honorable chap with his life marred by tragedy. Johnston had lost both his wife and his daughter. Julia Johnston's death was a matter of record, just as he described it to you."

"So you concentrated on Ariel Johnston."

"The doctor who signed the death certificate was her godfather. What if he'd falsified the document and Ariel Johnston hadn't died from a ruptured appendix? I checked the time sequence. Ariel had died shortly after Paul Foster had come down from Oxford and started to qualify at Guy's. Paul Foster was definitely a womanizer. Ergo, the good Dr. Brown had to be interrogated."

"Did Adam Kepesake go along with you?"

"He certainly agreed. As usual it was Brummell who did the actual work."

"At that point, Robby, did you suspect an abortion?"

"At that point I hadn't a clue. Brummell had his hands full with Dr. Brown. He insisted it was a matter of professional ethics, that his friend Matthew was a fine chap and wouldn't hurt a fly. It wasn't until Brummell showed the doctor the photos of the four bodies that he broke and told the truth. A few moments before I rang up to warn you that night, Beau Brummell and Kepesake came around to my flat. As soon as I spoke to you we headed for Maddersley at top speed." He added ruefully, "Which because of fog conditions was terribly slow. Sandy . . . I died a thousand deaths."

She bent her head and her voice was muffled. "So did I."

Putting out a hand, he covered her twitching one. "Why, after keeping everyone else at bay, did you let that man into the house?"

"I liked him and I wasn't . . . I felt no fear of him. There seemed no reason . . ."

"After I gave you his name and you decoyed him to the kitchen, why didn't you grab the baby and make a run for it?"

"I wasn't thinking that clearly. I couldn't believe my ears. All I could think of was to switch the cups just in case. For moments I thought you had made a mistake. Robby, I was a blind fool to trust him!"

"No," he told her gently. "At one time Johnston was a man worthy of trust. But he'd lived too long with loneliness, with hate, with pain for his only company. He had become twisted and obsessed. Remember this, Sandy. If Gillian Foster had been the way she appeared to him all this would never have happened. Johnston would never have harmed any of the Foster family. But Gillian, like so many idols, showed him feet of clay. Johnston went right over the brink."

They sat silently and then Miss Sanderson reached for the bottle. She knocked it over. As she righted it she giggled. "Good thing it's empty. Blimey, I've drained it and I'm feeling a little tiddly." She struggled to her feet. "Think I'd better go home. Aggie will be scandalized to see me in this condition."

He took her arm and steadied her. "She won't. We're leaving—"

"Chambers?"

"London. We're driving down to Sussex to the old family home for a few days. Wander out for long walks in good bracing air, eat Mrs. Meeks' delicious meals, and talk."

"But the work—"

"If young Peters and Vincent can't handle it they can shut up shop." He gave her a gentle push. "Into your washroom and scrub your face and tidy your hair. Then we're away."

She swayed and peered owlishly up at him. "Must remind me, Robby, got to buy a doll for little Lucy. For Christmas. Big, with ringlets and a ruffled petticoat. Will you help me?" Miss Sanderson asked.

"A doll like that must have a ruffled bonnet too. I'll help you, Sandy," Robert Forsythe promised.